The Eternal Feast
by BaronCroc

Adult Readers Only

This is a work of fiction. Any names or characters, businesses or places, events or incidents are fictitious and the products of the author's imagination. Any resemblance to actual persons, living or dead, or actual events is purely coincidental.

THE ETERNAL FEAST

Copyright © 2025 BaronCroc

All rights reserved.

Published by Bewere Books
Flagstaff, Arizona
https://www.bewere.net

ISBN: 978-1-62475-284-1
Printed in the United States, United Kingdom, or Australia
First trade paperback edition: December 2025

Cover art by BaronCroc
Edited by Cedric G. Bacon, Sandy Golden, and Packwolf Lupestripe

There are many things I want to say about this book. I want to talk ideas, inspiration and the furry fandom.

But instead, I'd like to say thanks. First of course to you, the one reading this! Thank you for purchasing my humble little story. But I also need to thank my friends in the fandom, all those who test-read, made artwork of Brock, role-played and chatted with me. I don't say enough how much you all mean.

Thank you, and enjoy the story!

Part 1

1. Changes

A darkness had fallen on Dachstaat.

Grimvald was the only one with the sense to notice.

When the king stood upon his fortress' high podium, a balcony looking out to courtyards and the city beyond, all came to bear witness. What an honour it was to hear the king's own words. Thousands packed themselves between those stone walls, even more so into the streets, their vision blocked by the buildings about them. Still in the height of summer, each and every rat could feel the warmth of the sun on their coats. Even if you couldn't hear from the bustle or the distance, a daisy-chain of voices carried in excited tones each word of King Hagan Brock the Mighty Crushing Paw's proclamation.

He stood, a great excess taller than any of his subjects upon a grey granite balcony. His figure always spoke to a life of plenty; plenty of strength in his tree-trunk legs, in his bulging arms that could lift a great sword like a twig, his chest, puffed proudly, an iron gut so that gravity dared not betray him. His eyes, orange, piercing, plenty keen on a black mask of fur, stark streaks of white to contrast. It was no doubt that he was a plenty handsome badger, to any rat you asked.

Plenty. That was what blindsided Grimvald on this day: the king in all his glorious conquest, had suddenly decided he'd had **plenty**.

"For on this day upon the Summer Solstice, I declare a new age! An era of peace for Dachstaat! We have proudly conquered all of the most bountiful land. Our strongest allies stand by our sides.

"Today, my people, we have **WON**!" The king's voice boomed, his growling timbre shaking Grimvald's ears as he stood by His Majesty's side like a dagger paired to a claymore. His eyes went wide and he turned swiftly to look to the distracted monarch as the people cried out:

"Long live the king!" The chanting seemingly went on forever.

Grimvald paced backwards, wrapping himself in his black cloak until only his grey face, pale pink nose, and ears penetrated the darkness.

His whole life had been in service as the king's trusted tactician, sleepless nights reading historical tomes in forgotten languages, taking hits from assassins, suffering a clawing scar across his face. Even then he himself was there to tend to the king's wounds before any other.

And now...now, was this how he would be betrayed? Tossed aside after a sudden thought of satisfaction?

It was the worst day of Marshal Grimvald Viletail's life.

He took off, away from the screaming crowds, away from the servants drinking merrily, away from the guards singing at their stations. He retreated to the southern tower, to his own quarters.

He called this tower home. War was everything, so as

the king's own tactician, he was granted these great quarters, shelves upon shelves of text upon text of any topic he demanded, as well as the finest drafting desk with the most gloriously crisp papers and metal writing tools made to his comfort. Within the few gaps between books were spoils of war, helms from the Gotter people that were moulded to the unique horns of each warrior, and claw caps from the Part'ah warriors who tried time and time again to ambush his soldiers in the night.

Looking over these fleeting things only served to deepen Grimvald's growing depression. Much like himself, they could all be tossed aside...

He wasn't the type to wallow in self-pity, but when faced with extinction, any man would take time to reflect on the beauty of what was now slipping away.

With his back against his door, he slumped to the ground with a thud. His bony hands wiped his nose, over his whiskers, across his narrowed eyes and finally slicked back his ears and the hair of his head. No, Grimvald was indeed **not** the type to give in so easily. There would still be the guard, royal or otherwise. All he had to do next was write an application to General Styl, or the Arcane Vicar. Congratulate them on their hard work, start building bridges towards his own smooth transition elsewhere.

Filled with a new determination, he scrambled to his feet and scurried over to the massive oak drafting table in his room. With a bit of fiddling with the table's angle for maximum comfort in writing, Grimvald took to neatly drawing out two nigh identical letters.

It was in his final moments of work, adding his signature flare to the crossed 't's' and dotted 'i's', that Grimvald heard a shuffle outside his chamber door. A small fist rapped the old wood a handful of times. It paused, then continued again with haste. Either impatience or fear.

Putting a sound to his frustration, a click of the tongue, the tactician stood, straightened his clothes, and approached the door, unlatching it and opening it partially in a single swift motion.

At first Grimvald thought he'd been made a fool, facing down an empty stairwell, but a castle link-boy cleared their throat, catching his attention.

"Yes?" Grimvald elongated the single word into a creaking question, his tail visibly swaying with an impatience that told the pup to keep it brief.

"I apologise for interrupting you at such a late hour. His Majesty wishes to see you sire."

Grimvald was surprised that the pup, pre-pubescent and shaking with nerves, didn't fuck up his sentence any further. Realising that he hadn't noticed the setting sun, Grimvald nodded to the link-boy and followed them downstairs.

If his time was up, he'd face it with dignity.

Down the spiralling tower, into the lengthy halls, Grimvald noted how quiet it was, and that he must've been sent a link-boy to allow the servants time to celebrate. Why else would you need a pup whose only job was to carry a torch in these well-lit halls? He could see everything but the topmost rafters which were lost by the light fading into obscurity.

Oh, but these halls. It was cliché to think, but they really could tell stories. Be it through the tapestries finely woven after grand battles, the shields and arms hung out of pride for those who'd fallen, or the literal tales upon manuscripts.

Something he particularly enjoyed as they approached the throne room were the portraits of the Brock family. One by one from the almost modern portrait of the king's own father all the way to the chipped and fading portrait of his great-great-great-grandmother. It was brought from the old country, the motherland of all badgers nestled far in the northern mountains. Sadly, the old country was rendered inhospitable by a 'lack of bounty', with all natural prey hunted to extinction. So, as every educated rat knows, the old inefficient democracy of Dachstaat was crushed by the merciful Brock family, bringing forth true leadership in the form of royalty.

Every member of the family proved themselves to be strong and noble rulers, with King Hagan Brock being the one who broke through the ancient impenetrable border wall of the Gotter people – a feat that his entire line had failed to achieve until Grimvald and he had concocted a plan to weaken its foundation. How they'd laughed as they mapped out a series of dams, re-routing an ocean of floodwater. They'd turned the enemy capital into little more than a swamp!

Grimvald's heart swelled with pride, with longing for those times past, as he left behind the link-boy and entered the throne room.

If you are to see the king, you are to see him on his terms, at his best, his most his most impactful, imposing. You enter the two main doors that connect to the entrance of the building and see a grand long line of royal guards along a gilded carpet. This leads to a large dark vespin-wood throne, deep black with stark white veins, and on that throne a strong figure. A simple glance from him is enough to make you grovel at his feet.

But, with familiarity comes expediency. Grimvald always entered the throne room from a door to the king's left, a short walk to his side, and a practised bow that left little space for him to scan the monarch's mood. In this moment, the king was staring deeply into a chalice of pyment in his paws, swirling it about in a small whirlpool. He must've been at this for some time; Grimvald could smell the spring berries on the air.

"How might I serve you, Your Majesty?" He decided to break the silence sooner rather than later. Brock seemed to be in one of his more serious moods. It was best to cut through the indecision and get to the meat.

"Exactly..." Gripping the chalice firmly, Brock cut the pyment's trajectory, causing a few drops to fly onto the stone floor beyond the throne. "You've always possessed a good mind for the future, Grimvald." The king's voice in this moment, as it was in all private moments they had, was characteristically deep and husky, lacking any of the aggression he would show to others. "You have obviously realised by now your work is unnecessary in a peaceful Dachstaat. But I can't have you displaced from the castle, living on the street, can I?"

"It would indeed be a waste sir." He said calmly.

"A waste!" With a toast to that choice of words, Brock continued. "Indeed, Grimvald. So I have come to a decision. I shall have you as a royal advisor. In fact..." The king sat back some, kicking a foot to prop up upon his thigh. "...I'm going to hold a feast tomorrow. Hell, I may even continue the celebrations into the next day. Who's to say I won't continue into the day after that!" The king grinned.

"As I will be indisposed with celebration and such, I'd like you, Grimvald, to make sure the castle runs smoothly without my intervention. I don't want to be interrupted.

"Is that understood?" Brock's grin faded suddenly upon that final sentence, his expression dark, snout tilted down.

Grimvald's tail went stiff as a broom, his hands, behind his back, gripped tightly at the shift in intensity. He often forgot that the king was a carnivore. In another life, the Brock family may have chosen to dine on his kind.

"Of course, Your Majesty. I shall make sure your feast is uninterrupted."

"Ha! Brilliant!" The king slapped his knee with his free paw before knocking back his drink and swiftly getting to his feet. "I shall get plenty of rest then. In the meantime, make sure the staff are ready for a **full day** of feasting tomorrow!"

With the chalice shoved into Grimvald's paws, the king walked with a surprisingly steady gait from the throne room towards his private quarters. He knew the king could put away his drink easily, but by the bottles lined in a row beside the throne, it would not take a seer to surmise he had been drinking for some while, alone with only his thoughts. Despite all that time to think, Grimvald had no answers as to the sudden change of heart towards warfare. But it was something he could ask the king after his feast had concluded.

With a sigh of relief and a quick shake to remove the tension that filled him, Grimvald left to forewarn the staff of their upcoming gauntlet.

King Hagan Brock was no stranger to feasts. They were a normal part of life in the castle, especially as the result of a victory. If the king felt it necessary, he would even celebrate the achievements of his people, inviting the architects and foremen who created great fortresses and libraries, or entertainers who he wished to witness first-hand, letting them eat and rest before a day of performance around the castle. The throne room was indeed large enough that even jugglers on horse-back could gallop about and perform from the safety of the castle walls. A tightrope was even once deployed between two of the outer towers so the king may see a true show of bravery. Although, that was a terrible example; the goddesses of the wind had not let that performance end well.

So performers came, jesters, musicians, dancers, anyone who had previously impressed His Majesty to dance and sing, one by one in a great procession as the monarch with his top brass drank and ate all manner of delicacies.

Birds stuffed into other birds who had been fed only the finest herbs and grain, root vegetables roasted with sea salt and honey, cuts of steak swimming in butter that practically melted in the mouth, whole pigs turning slowly in the centre of the room. The desserts were also to die for, and chocolate flowed more generously than water. What a boastful display, after the acquisition of so much tropical land, to offer not only these delicacies but a great wealth of fruit on display.

This of course, as the king had warned, did not transpire over a single day.

No; almost as regularly as the entertainers came and went, so did the guests. While most of them were nobility or the king's trusted knights and generals, a scant few common folk were chosen by raffle to enjoy leftovers by the plateful in the courtyard of the castle. It was an astounding kindness, one that would have taken Grimvald by surprise if he had been paying attention.

The king himself was almost always present. He would leave only to sleep when it became too late to continue, or to freshen himself up at mid-day. In feasts past, especially the ones that lasted more than three days, the king would become absent for a day in-between. On the third he would disappear to swing his rusty sword arm, sleep and bathe, then return on the fourth to continue or conclude.

But it was as if the king had been starved his entire life.

Now he was unstoppable. Not a single dish was spared as he steadily ate. In fact, the only times he refrained from stuffing something into his mouth were the moments when he would quip at the expense of a stumbling juggler, between courses, or if there was no food left for him to eat.

Most importantly, if there was food on the table, Brock was there too.

Grimvald, as was always the case, ate on the first day and then every third afterwards.

He enjoyed his figure and despised mess. It was also within his best interest to watch the table for Brock, especially now that he was under new orders and greater responsibilities. He spent the first days keeping the staff in order, reminding them of their duties when they fell behind, and made sure each and every guest was seen to. It ceased being tiring work when a rhythm was found, and it stopped being work when the number of guests gradually dwindled.

This gave the advisor ample time to observe his king, to untangle the knot before him.

Over the week Brock did not slow, and he paid less and less attention to his surroundings. By the second day, his stomach was round and taut. By the fourth it sat squarely on his lap, a softness forming where it hung downwards, and by the sixth there was a noticeable plumpness to his upper limbs and sides.

Grimvald almost felt it appropriate to intervene – Brock was obviously feeling pain from this marathon. His breathing laboured as the day grew long, and he'd power through a wince whenever he would lean forward for more.

But he refrained. These feasts were a week at most, so he kept up the king's order. He was not to be interrupted. Grimvald was sure that after the seventh day, all would return to normal.

"Good morning, Your Majesty, would you care to join me for a walk around the courtyard?" Grimvald spoke after knocking upon the heavy ornate door to Brock's bedroom. The royal advisor held a small ledger in his paws, as he was sure he would for many of the days to come. This one was given to him mere minutes prior by the head accountant, Sir Archibald. It was a worrying sight, but something that would be easily balanced now that the financial drain of conducting war was no longer an issue.

There was no reply... Grimvald furrowed his snout in concern. The king had definitely not exited his room. He confirmed so with the morning staff.

He knocked again, waited, then heard a grumble on the other side of the door.

"Enter!" Brock called out, a gummy growl to his voice.

Without hesitation, Grimvald did as he was told, but quickly averted his eyes upwards.

The king was sitting at the side of his massively excessive bed, fully in the nude, a sour look upon his face. His gut, seemingly still round from the late night before, growled loudly before the king unabashedly let out what felt like a 30-second belch.

Grimvald flinched at the sudden noise and flash of teeth, his ears falling back as it continued.

Seemingly, by his expression, the king felt better after that uncouth display. After clearing his throat, Brock spoke as he stood with a grunt of effort.

"You spoke of a walk, Grimvald?"

"Yes, Your Majesty," He replied swiftly. "Once concluded I have organised a quick but hearty breakfast followed by a meeting wi-"

"Ha! I did not know you **could** tell jokes!" On his feet, the king snapped his teeth when he interrupted the rat, who was four feet below his gaze. He was not a small man before his feasting, that was obvious to all. But while taller than most rats, Grimvald was still a toothpick in comparison to the tree before him. He took a step back, away from the king's advance.

He did not shake or cower when he spoke. No, Grimvald had been at the receiving end of Brock's frustration before. He simply directed his gaze downwards in reverence and made sure to ask the correct question. "My apologies sire. What did you have in mind for today?"

"As I had instructed you, Grimvald. I never said the feast was over! You shall continue your good work, make sure I am not interrupted."

"I..." What? "I, of course." Was he asleep? He must be asleep. Or did he miss a day of the week? Grimvald quickly flipped open the ledger in his paws... It had indeed been seven days.

"Sir I have no guests to join you for the feast, is-"

"That's fine, Grimvald! I shall eat alone, or..." Out of the advisor's sight, King Brock stared at himself in the mirror, his large dark paw gently pressed from his navel to his side. It was just that little bit softer than yesterday. As was everything else. "Hm. Get me my tailor, have her staff adjust my doublet, breeches and knickerbockers. **Then**, invite them to eat with me!" Brock had a wide grin on his face as he stroked his beard. Oh, so proud he was at this idea.

"If nobody comes after that, I eat alone."

"Understood, sir." While he tried his hardest to hide his displeasure, Grimvald couldn't help but let a small grumble slip through. 'One more day,' he told himself.

"They shall be with you momentarily, sir," Grimvald spoke before bowing and swiftly exiting the room. First, he'd alert the kitchen staff. Shiloh was sure to have some massive opinions on this development.

2. The Staff

The kitchen staff were not happy. Shiloh especially. As the Steward of the castle's culinary wing, Shiloh Thistlesting was drowning in work the last week, her only respite being that the days following would be quieter. All the castle recovering from their food comas, it was time to take stock, order more food, let the staff take a half day. But no... Grimvald entering the kitchens, ordering **her** staff. That was a step too far— she could handle the king's demands for a further day of feasting, but not that snooty backstabber crossing into her territory.

The ensuing argument was short, with an agreement set down by the head chef. She didn't want any further noise in her kitchen. Shiloh would get on with the king's feast, and Grimvald would cool off and meet her in a few hours in the portrait room.

So, as agreed, the tailors made it to the king, and once he was able to fit into his clothes once more, all of them returned to the main dining hall for a round of pastries, eggs of all descriptions, sausages and any type of cured meat the staff could find.

Like most any space in the castle the portrait room was ostentatious. Contrary to its name, it was not a room filled with portraits; it was a room used once in a generation to **paint** portraits. Backdrops by the dozens were found stored here displaying adventurous vistas, calming seaside escapes and conquered foreign lands all from the comfort of this room. The pageantry on display added verve to each piece, showing the personality of the Explorer, Sailor and Warrior, as well as comfortable seating for the reigning monarch to perch upon while being sketched and painted. At any other time, it was used by certain high-ranking members of the staff to parlay. While most of them got along as well as peers and contemporaries might be expected to, there were moments like this where neutral ground and privacy was required.

Grimvald was already present when Shiloh arrived. She opened the door exactly as wide as it was needed for her to stride through. She was not slight like Grimvald, but far from an ample figure. She was the vision of a mother, strict and uncompromising, past middle-age yet not a scar or imperfection upon her. Her fur was dust grey and her ears bright and rosy, and of her entrance she was in possession of a confident strut with a black cane in her left hand, something she was not seen without, either to support her stride or strike anyone who mistreated her underlings.

She couldn't help but roll her eyes at the sight of him, legs crossed on a footboard bench, perfect posture and a focused glare upon his face.

"Grimvald," she stated.

"Shiloh," Grimvald commented, gesturing his nose towards a chair across from himself.

She simply stood beside it. "Let's make this quick, I

have thirty minutes until the jester runs out of new material."

"Fine." Grimvald shifted, crossing his legs in the opposite direction. "You're not a fool Shiloh, so I will assume you have noticed the king's irrational behaviour."

"I've noticed a slightly longer than usual feast. Maybe he **really** likes the food." Shiloh, frustrated, moved to exit, but Grimvald's next words made her pause.

"He's never held these feasts for himself. They were for the noble financiers, for the generals and the people praying that they would get to eat the same food the king nibbled upon. **You** know that. It was always a show. So, if nobody is here, if there are no witnesses, what does that mean?"

She stopped for a beat and thought upon his question. "I don't know, Grimvald. What **does** it mean?"

"I can only assume that he's snapped, and this is some sort of a... a bout of insanity." He was scrambling for an answer, anything that would make this make sense. "We must help our king, mustn't we?"

He lost composure for just long enough that Shiloh felt a tiny little pang of empathy for Grimvald. A tactician with no fight? She supposed this was the best he had. The least she could do was keep him busy.

"Grimvald, You should discuss this with Shaw," she said, leaning against the closed door with her arms crossed and her cane tapping against her side. He clearly did not know Shaw, so Shiloh continued. "Shaw is the royal herbalist, dabbles in medicine, alchemy. She's not been needed aside from producing painkillers, so if you're looking for something to settle his addled mind, I'm sure she can help." She would surely be looking for a new project to keep her busy.

After but a second to assure that Grimvald had no further questions, Shiloh clicked her fingers when Grimvald's eyes wandered. "You owe **me** for my time and my staff for their unwavering service. See to it that they are compensated." With that she slipped out of the room, barely making a noise aside from the door shutting behind her.

A sigh broke the silence. Grimvald had only heard about Shaw in whispers. Rumours that did not bode well for anyone involved.

King Hagan Brock's grandmother, Queen Aphelia Brock, adored topiary animals. One was brought to her in a massive ornate pot as part of a gift from an empire that wished to trade with Dachstaat. With that simple gesture she was hooked, and so the queen took the empire by force just to have the artisans that created these living sculptures under her thumb.

So out behind the inner sanctum of Hordrigg Castle the facade of efficient brutality was thrown on its head by a majestic garden consumed by all manners of wild flower, berry bush and creeping vine.

If the king wasn't so distracted now that he was spending so much time in the castle he may have glanced outside and seen this mess of unkempt foliage and demanded it flattened. But here, and now, it was where Shaw, the castle's herbalist spent every hour. living in a shed and divvying out her concoctions to anyone who dared approach.

Gimvald was never a fan of 'nature'. He enjoyed the occasional hunt in the appropriate gear, sure, but at the king's side, his way was usually cleared of branches and stinging thorns. He audibly exclaimed in disgust when his boot became sullied by a splatter of mud.

'It's for the greater good,' he muttered inaudibly to himself as he vaulted a low stone wall and approached the shed he was hunting for. The building was surprisingly sturdy looking, a cabin of half logs, moss and packed mud. If the vines and lichen were stripped from its walls, he might've been impressed by the workmanship.

Before Grimvald could knock at the door, it suddenly shot open several inches, catching the advisor off guard enough that he hopped back a pace and put a paw upon the dagger at this side.

"Greetings!" called a squat curly-furred rat. She bruxed her teeth fervently in a way that made her large eyes bulge.

"Shaw, is it?" Grimvald did his best to keep a straight face.

"Aye, yes! That's me." With a joyous confirmation she stood, hands on hips, looking at her visitor with a smile. He noted the thick leather apron and gloves she was equipped with, as well as a toolbelt of all manner of equipment. Shears, pincers, measuring cups on strings, water bladders and blades.

After a moment more waiting for an expected social queue, Grimvald felt it appropriate to continue the conversation in her stead.

"I'm Grimvald Viletail, we have not met. As of a week ago I have been acting as the king's royal advisor and temporary liaison in facilitating the celebrations currently unfolding..." As he spoke at length, her expression faded into a blank stare. "...You are aware of the celebrations, aren't you?"

"Oh yes, probably!" During her cheerful claim she shook her head.

"Right, I see... May we have this conversation inside?"

"Yeah, why not?" Ever enthusiastic, Shaw turned and left the partially open door behind her as she dropped onto her bed, which sat across from a long bench overflowing with bottles, bowls and burners. Two of the latter produced a steady flame under some in-progress concoction.

The rest of the room was just as chaotic: festoons of hanging leaves, dried fish, flowers by the bushel, and an entire brightly-coloured (dead) snake.

Grimvald simply stood in the centre of the room as to not disturb anything. "So, as you may... Or may not know, the king has been holding a feast the last seven days. As of today, the eighth, said feast has continued. This, obviously, is very unlike him, and I am under the impression from his behaviour that His Majesty is not of his right mind. From what I have been told, you are particularly skilled in creating tinctures. Perhaps you could create something that could help him find peace in his addled state."

Grimvald paused and tucked his chin to his chest as a thought crossed his mind. "We cannot have it be obvious, you see. He's never been the type to forgive meddling behind his back, even if it is for his own good... Perhaps we could disguise the tincture as a remedy for indigestion or bloat or somesuch. He did mention some gastric discomfort..." Grimvald trailed off, brows furrowed and a finger to his lips as he pondered their options.

Shaw had her pinkie finger scratching about in one of her ears while he'd been speaking. Upon realising he was done talking, she quickly hopped to her feet and clapped her hands. Grimvald, once again caught off guard, jumped where he stood.

"I understand you exactly, sir!"

"Y-you do?" Grimvald replied, perplexed.

"Yes! I'll start with a base of a cure for his upset stomach, make it convincing... but his hunger is the issue, yes? That must be the solution! We'll k-"

"What a brilliant idea!" Out of sheer excitement for the end of this ordeal, he interrupted her explanation. "We shall thwart his celebrations through his hunger!" The advisor clapped his hands twice, a grin showing for a moment. "You have my go-ahead Shaw, just be sure to test this brew before you offer it to the king."

"Yes sir!" She gave a salute, chest puffed, wrong hand, an odd look on her face.

"Don't ever do that again."

By Grimvald's order the doors to the banquet hall were closed to all but the kitchen staff for the rest of the day. It was much easier than keeping a watchful eye on him like a mischievous child.

It was not an issue until just before dinner when the castle accountant, Archibald, arrived at the hall doors a moment after Shaw was escorted in by the advisor himself.

"I assume I must await my turn." Archibald, portly, thick in the tail and the neck, wore shades of red white and gold as he always did. He was born in nobility and it thoroughly showed. He was planning on speaking to the king on her behalf, but that was obviously off the table now. He ran some claws through his light grey fur, preening himself despite Grimvald's succinct shake of the head.

"The king will not be interrupted today. I am under strict orders to take on any incoming matters. So, spit it out." He kept an even, displeased tone. Archibald knew of Grimvald's promotion, yet didn't seem to get the message.

"Ah, well. From what I understand, the celebrations are continuing despite the lack of attendees. While we are spending less due to the lack of individuals, the king still requires entertainers as he eats, and he still expects the same spread at every meal. We must conci-"

"I'm well ahead of you, Archibald, and I have the situation under control. Is there anything else?"

"Oh! Splendid. Well, the treasury of course looks healthy, but if we wish to keep it that way he must consider opening trade with one of the nations within the scaled alliance. Perhaps a meeting could be set to discuss terms? Obviously, that is a future matter, so I will prepare the necessary documentation and funding for travel at a leisurely pace.

Ah, hm, I suppose that is **all,** Mr. Grimvald." He looked quite satisfied.

The advisor nodded and gestured for Archibald to exit, to which, a tad bewildered, the accountant did so. It was not as if he'd brought anything to light that Grimvald wasn't already contending with.

Once Archibald was out of sight, Grimvald felt brave enough to hold his ear against the door to the banquet hall. It would be out of order for him to interrupt right this moment, but he would rather not be left out of the loop.

The voices were muffled and distant, and any overheard sentence had to be deciphered.

'You...your name is...Shaw, is it? What did you put in this?'

'Ah! Ginger, Fire bark, Yuzu rind-'

Just as she listed off the ingredients, Grimvald stood straight, acting inconspicuous when a pair of guards marched by. They were slow and, unfortunately for Grimvald, they were doing their job correctly, giving a proper salute as they passed him...

Once they out of sight he tilted his head once more... "Ha! Curious. If this works, I'll be sure to call upon you again, Shaw."

When he could hear Shaw's approaching footsteps he crept backwards as to not be seen from the hall, only speaking up once the doors were securely shut.

"So?" Grimvald sidled up to Shaw, looming over her.

"He **loved** it! I had to be careful with the dose as I've not adjusted for a badger with such a brew before, but we should see how it goes by breakfast tomorrow."

"Wonderful, wonderful. Good work, Shaw. You are dismissed." With a pat on her shoulder, Grimvald turned to face the banquet hall's doors. After a few moments, Shaw got the message and scurried off.

With a deep clear breath and the reassurance in his mind that all would return to normal soon, Grimvald continued to redirect anyone who might bother the king.

The rest of the day went as expected. King Brock ate, demanded a suitable dessert, and, once he was stuffed to the brim, dismissed the musicians present and meandered his way to his quarters. He was definitely a worrying sight; Grimvald couldn't help but lag behind and spy on his king. His sturdy stride was replaced by an unbalanced sway, his gut groaning as the occasional burp escaped him. With his doublet unbuttoned long ago, his large black furred gut, peppered by long grey hairs, swayed ahead of him. That new softness had only grown more pronounced, as it seemed even his sleeves were getting tight. A rip could be heard when he lifted an arm to steady himself on a wall. If he kept going like this...

No.

As the royal herbalist, Shaw, had earned her position,

surely. There was to be no more feasting after this. Her concoction would kill his hunger, and he would call off the celebrations in the morning. Maybe sleep off his food until mid-day, then resume his training regime.

As Grimvald left for his tower, he found a new pep to his step.

The king had demanded breakfast be served to him in his quarters.

When Grimvald received this news, he was unsure of what to think. Hell, he was unsure of what to **do**. He needed more information, but the last time he'd questioned the king's actions had not gone smoothly. Grimvald elected instead to observe.

In doing so, he observed the king make several more demands for food to be brought to him. Then he took leave for a nap, departing his quarters in an unbuttoned shirt and doublet with an order for staff to move a table into the throne room. Grimvald watched the king situate himself on his large plush throne. This was not questioned by the staff, but Grimvald could only assume that the king wished to eat sooner, and the throne room was ever so slightly closer to his quarters than the banquet hall.

Highly, highly disturbing news. Yet when Grimvald voiced his dissatisfaction to Shaw, she simply assured him that they could up the dose safely until he was happy.

So the king was given another dose. He happily took it and continued as normal the next day, so Shaw suggested another, then another the next day.

"It's **not** working." Grimvald spoke through his teeth, his rage clear. He'd confronted her just after Brock woke, holding her by the apron near her throat against an overgrown shoulder-height wall out in the garden.

She was not very good at hiding her fear when he pushed her harder against the stone. She stammered as her eyes darted from the advisor to the blade ever at his side. "I-It's working perfectly, is it not!?"

"What the **fuck** could you possibly mean!?" He was not one to raise his voice, but these were especially frustrating circumstances.

"The tincture! The br-brew increases hunger, bolsters the stomach..."

"**WHAT!!?**" Grimvald felt faint, his head spun as he let go of Shaw. Immediately he stumbled back and steadied himself on the opposite wall.

Shaw, collecting herself, offered the advisor her water skin. After a pause to catch his breath, he accepted. "I'm very sorry sir; did you **not** want to take the throne? With the way you were talking I really thought... I suppose it's a bit convoluted to fatten the king to weaken him..."

He was going insane. Grimvald sank to the floor, not even caring about the muck he found himself sitting in. He sat simply, wide eyed and in astonishment. Before he fully checked out for the day, Grimvald was somehow able to mutter out a plea: "Shaw, you cannot mention any of this to anyone."

3. Supply and Commands

After a subsequent meeting, Shaw agreed to only provide the king with what he knew he was getting: a tonic for indigestion. Anything else was to be left **out**.

Unfortunately for Grimvald, this did not seem to slow down King Brock's increasing hunger, nor the slowly growing demand of his stomach. Ever so gradually, day by day, the king would eat a little more. This lessened the leftovers for the staff, and by consequence created a larger order to refill the larder each week. Before the feasts they would refill the larder by the month. A month after the first week of feasting, they experienced their first incident.

Grimvald only witnessed the aftermath, picking up the details in the following hours. The king had been part way through his dinner, taking a break to enjoy the festivities. During this time the servants entered to claim their share as they traditionally would. They took what was on offer: crumbly crusts of bread, gristly bones, and the dregs of the soup. But as they scraped together a shared meal it became very apparent that they had used up the last of the food, leaving nothing else for the king.

One of the servers made the terrible mistake of taking the kitchen's issue directly to the king while Grimvald was using the garderobe.

They said something along the lines of: "I regret to inform you, sir, that the pantry is fully depleted."

To which the king huffed, and Grimvald could only assume what was said in reply: "Well, bring back what you just cleared," believing it to be an easy task.

The server explained: "Your Majesty, that food has been given to the staff."

What happened next varied depending on whom you asked.

Some claimed that the king shoved them aside and ordered them to simply find **anything** for him.

Others claimed that he grabbed the server and demanded that the food be pulled from the mouths of the staff and brought back to him.

The least likely and most ridiculous was that the poor fellow was eaten on the spot! This was simply disproven when Grimvald spied the shocked individual sipping a lukewarm cup of broth in the solar.

After a quick word with a different server, Grimvald confirmed that the staff were just about able to provide the king's desserts, so, as much as he dreaded confronting King Brock in such a mood, he thought it best to reassure him that sustenance was on the way.

Grimvald entered the throne room out of Brock's sight, but instinctively retreated when a loud clatter frightened him.

The jester, adorned in a motley outfit in both sound and colour, had barely dodged the projectile. The steak knife loudly clattered against the wall behind where the jester had been jingling miserably. The jester rose to his feet and, with tears in his eyes, tried a different approach to distract the impatient king. He began clutching his chest as if the king had hit him, and dramatically throwing about all manner of objects from various sleeves and pockets before falling to the floor.

The king cracked a slight smile, less out of actual entertainment and more from the thought of having harmed this unlucky entertainer.

Grimvald, hoping to save all present from any further displeasure, cleared his throat.

Brock swiftly turned his head where he sat and called out with a sickening grin: "Grimmy! Just who I wished to talk to." Compared to the month prior, the king was a parody of himself. Upon a throne he used to spread himself across, his thighs and bulging waistline completely filled the seat. Even his chest now sat upon his stomach, which covered the majority of his lap. As he raised his flagon of mead to the approaching advisor his arm showcased a new jiggle that covered what used to be rock hard muscle. Maybe Grimvald wouldn't have felt as offended if his clothes were not so ill-fitting. His shirt was fully unbuttoned, and Gimvald could see at least one had flown off and now sat under the table.

The king continued before Grimvald approached.

"You must speak to the kitchen staff, they're slacking." He snapped.

"I came to apologise on their behalf sir." As he spoke, Grimvald waved a hand at the jester (who was still 'dying' on the floor) to exit. Grimvald then sat himself on the dining table, side saddle, hands on his propped-up thigh. "The larder is completely cleared a day earlier than expected. **Including** the reserves. They are preparing your dessert at this very moment."

"Ah! Already ahead of me." He seemed to cheer up a moment before his expression went dark once more, "You don't think they've done this on purpose, do you?"

"No, sir." He almost bit his tongue in trying to hide how he felt about this possibility.

The king grinned, taking his bulging gut in both paws, he did not lift it so much as rubbed the sides upwards. This was punctuated by a slap to the side of the most laut-looking part of his stomach. "I'll tell you, old friend, there is no better feeling than finally eating like the king I am! Have we not earned such luxury? Earned **any** life we desire?"

Grimvald's nose scrunched up out of instinct at this display.

Brock would have continued his thought immediately, but stifled a belch before he could. "What do you want, Grimvald? While we wait, tell me what **you** want." The king leaned forward towards Grimvald, or as much as his stomach allowed him. He had his flagon poking into his advisor's chest to goad a reply from him. When Grimvald looked down at the sloshing cup it raised to push his chin upwards.

"I..." What could he say? I want the only warrior I look up to to return to his old ways? Looking at Brock in this moment, he saw he was... happy. Brock would smile in the past, sure, they would joke as they rode across the countryside, but that was a shadow compared to the beaming smile upon his maw when he held his gut moments earlier.

"...I want to continue serving you, sir." His eyes darted away after only a second of eye contact. He could see a somewhat unsure, but gentle, smile upon Brock's face.

The king chuckled, scratching his neck absently as he sat back and situated himself more comfortably on his seemingly shrinking chair. "I suppose that was the **correct** answer. Hm. Well! If you think of something else, you take what you desire from the treasury. We have a wealth of strong horses I will not be riding any time soon, too! Ha!" Brock, adoring his own joke, laughed heartily. As was instinctual, Grimvald laughed too.

When dessert arrived Grimvald slipped into the background, as Brock enjoyed his fill of pastries, cakes, fruits, and pies, the advisor sampled a selection of fresh berries and watched his king eat.

The next day, the kitchen's shipment was late; thankfully not enough that the castle would miss King Brock's breakfast, but it was close, with dishes being staggered as they were finished. Eggs were being taken straight from the bushel and into pans, pastries and bread being served last as soon as they were baked. New chickens for the castle's eggs were even purchased, as the previous ones had to be butchered to keep up with last night's demands.

As the staff joked about feeding the poultry whole to the king, Shiloh spotted Grimvald approaching the kitchens. She wasn't angry, at least not this time. When she spotted him, he seemed to be double-checking the incoming shipment against the order paperwork, a job which was otherwise neglected in the panic.

She did quickly remember why she should be angry.

Grimvald hadn't lived up to his end of their deal.

The speed at which Shiloh walked towards the other was alarming enough that he lost his place in counting links of sausages and took a step back in preparation.

But she did not yell at him, did not hit him with her cane, nor did she even frown.

She simply said: "You still owe me."

Grimvald raised a brow, then followed up by rolling the papers in his hands into a tight bunch and smiled. "**I** owe you? I would think **you** owe **me**." He tapped the roll of papers against a crate to his right in a small percussive tune. As he continued, he dragged out his words, finding joy in each. "I saved your ass."

"How?" She was obviously insulted.

Grimvald offended Shiloh even more by pointing his wand of papers at her face as he spoke. "The king wished to **punish** your staff for not providing him his feast in full and I convinced him not to. We're at the very **least** even." He retracted the papers, but only after she smacked them aside.

"No we are not. Do you know the strings I had to pull, the favours I've had to call, to get this shipment together early? I don't think you even realise how much shit I've had to wade through to keep this feast, that **you** said was 'under your control', staffed and stocked for **all this fucking time!**" Now Shiloh was the one doing the pointing, she took her cane and stuck it right at Grimvald's chest. "You still owe me. Increased pay as long as this continues."

He grabbed her cane and used it to push her back two paces. The kitchen staff slowed to watch the power struggle; the background chatter had faded at least a minute ago.

Grimvald replied, cold and emotionless, "You will get **nothing**." He punctuated by pushing the cane aside before exiting the kitchen.

Shiloh stared in silence as Grimvald left, but once he was out of sight, she clapped her hands and called out for the staff to get the king's breakfast finished.

A number of things were to be sorted after breakfast. The king was to be measured for his doublet to be expanded, then as the tailors retrieved the needed fabrics and worked, the king was to speak with Archibald. After that, and once he was properly clothed, he had requested to see some jousting in the courtyard.

It felt as if the joust came out quickly. The horses were out, the knights in full regalia, and the stage set. A number of nobility and warriors of renown had come to watch. Even Archibald had come, taking an undeserved break from his engagements. Grimvald, having been out in the yard after breakfast, hadn't seen the accountant in some time, and to his dismay had noted that he must've been joining the king to eat more often. He sported an even fuller face, and his belt strained when he sat amongst the nobles.

But the king... was nowhere to be found.

The moment he realised he was missing, Grimvald hurried indoors once more, only to see the king upon the stairs that connected to the entrance hall, slowly meandering his way down.

"Ah, your highness." He spoke, catching his attention.

Brock was wearing a beloved combination: silk hose, a great golden jewelled chain atop a fur-lined coat, and a doublet which was fastened tight with two belts. Those belts went a long way toward allowing his legs better range of motion.

"Yes, yes, Grimvald, I'm coming," he said with a pinch of frustration as he slowly approached. Now that he was unable to see the steps below him, the king carefully guided himself by the railing and touch, but, thankfully, made it safely to the bottom without assistance.

Grimvald took a deep breath, relieved, and walked alongside Brock to guide him to his seat. "Your Highness, everything is in order, and all are awaiting your arrival to begin."

Together, they emerged from the castle's grand doorway and were met both by the applause of the common people, and quiet, rippling murmurs among them. Thankfully for their own sakes the sound of polite clapping and 'huzzahs' blocked out the buzz of concerned chatter, amused conversation and outright gasps.

At this point the king was larger than last seen by the public, but not far beyond previous monarchs or even foreign leaders in recent history.

While his stomach did sag, the belts, as Grimvald had already noted, did make it appear as if he was no larger comparatively to the largest noblemen, content to sit about with a lifetime of rich foods. Though, the only truly unclothed part of the king's body, his neck and head, did betray him. His once angular and chiselled jawline had softened to such a degree that his neck quaked and trembled as he went forward. Worse, his slow, ponderous pace saw the audience's applause drop off until only the most devoted kept their hands aloft. By the time the king arrived at his chair upon a lifted stage, the crowd, exhausted, had fallen silent. At this point, King Brock's laboured breath could be heard by those nearby. Pages hid their faces or kept their shocked expressions to themselves. There came the sound of the steps below him creaking angrily as he took a tight hold of the guard rail to his left. One step, then the second, then a third at a time, stopping for a moment before he attempted the fourth. His descent earlier, combined with this walk outside, had been the most exercise the king had engaged with in over a month.

So, while the pause he took was understandable, Grimvald still had to work hard to not look horrified at this. The thought finally crossed his mind: with the direction Brock was going in...

With a final creak of bending wood, the king all but collapsed into his seat and called out "Commence!" in his characteristic, all-consuming voice.

To which, of course, all chattering ended, and the riders mounted their steeds, shuttering their helmets for a lap of the arena before the game commenced.

The performance went without issue, likely as all King Brock had to do was sit and be provided drink. But Grimvald could see his impatience growing and mood darkening. Usually when Brock's face scrunched so, he was bored and needed some action, but he was currently watching two men trading blows and being thrown from horses, so it could not be boredom.

By the sunlight upon the walls surrounding them, at least an hour had passed since the king arrived. In the next fifteen minutes, Brock and his visitors would be served lunch in the banquet hall. Realising that Brock would soon start to complain, Grimvald excused himself quietly and hurried himself inside and towards the kitchens in search of Shiloh.

It was out of the ordinary for him to talk to the staff before a meal to ensure all was running smoothly, especially since this new way of life had truly settled in for all working in the castle. But on this day with guests joining for luncheon, Grimvald could feel something rotten in his tail, an ill omen. A terrible feeling that only grew worse as he walked the halls.

There was nobody to be found.

Utter silence fell upon Castle Hordrigg, as the guards were attending the joust; not even the routine clanking of armaments could be heard.

But as he arrived in the kitchens his blood truly went cold, his heart rate rose, and his eyes went wild.

There was nothing on the fire, no fires going, just empty pots and pans, and produce in storage, untouched. Not a single person was in the kitchens.

Grimvald gritted his teeth and called out for Shiloh as he hurried down the halls towards the servants' quarters. As he walked the few who crossed his path cowered with their hands aloft as they begged for his mercy. Not for any fear of him, no. They looked to him for protection, and they were still useful to Grimvald as long as the king was hungry. But Shiloh? She held no pity in her heart for honest workers. She looked only for loyalty in her staff and would pull every string at her disposal to punish a traitor.

When he saw her, Shiloh was at the door to the servant's quarters. It was open ajar, all of the kitchen staff must have heard his rage coming from a mile away. Those closest peeked through the gap, until his arrival caused the door to shut suddenly, leaving just the two of them in the corridor to collide.

"Shiloh, you coward." He spoke venomously, a hand on the dagger at his side as he stood just far enough away that if she did strike out with her cane, she would not have a chance to disarm him. "You stage some half-brained strike right **now,** when the top brass come to visit!? When the king will hunger most?"

"What better time to let **you** know how serious we are?" she sneered. She thought she was smart; Grimvald could see it in the smile she held when she spoke, arms crossed, so casually perched. Oh, how wrong she was.

Grimvald's lips curved into the shadow of a snarl. "You'll be seriously dead if you don't have something ready in the next twenty minutes." His grave tone did not cause her to waver.

"Dead!? Grimvald, don't make me laugh! The king will throw a fork at you and demand you give us whatever we wish the moment I speak my piece." She wasn't even looking at him now, her confidence through the roof. That was until Grimvald spoke again.

"You'll be in pieces if you don't **wake up** Shiloh." He pointed at her, square in the chest, his fur on end and tail raised. "You think he won't threaten the staff with execution and have **you** served for lunch? It wouldn't be hard at all for me to find a new kitchen staff from any business in this city."

"He wouldn't." Oh, how she second guessed what she just said. He could see it in how tense she became at his words, how her pose shifted to a defensive stance, almost ready to bolt.

"Oh, he would. You think he hasn't already threatened those more replaceable than you? Do you really think at the rate he is going he wouldn't make an example? I have his ear, Shiloh, and trust me when I say does that go both ways." He took a step closer. "The king has said some unsavoury things about how similar rat meat is to rabbit."

Her brows furrowed and nose twitched. "Fine." Her ears drooped for but a moment before she regained her composure. "Keep him waiting for five minutes."

"Good." Grimvald said. Just as silently as he had unsheathed it, he replaced his blade and made his way back to the king.

The lunch service was slow to start. But Grimvald expected as such. Fresh fruit and berries, cheeses, preserved meats and buttered bread to nibble upon as the real meal was prepared. But even with little time to prepare, the portion sizes were more than enough to satisfy this gathering.

The advisor was quite proud of himself, and with cheese in hand he toasted proudly to Shiloh as she stood in the wings.

Shiloh claimed her revenge in her own way in the coming weeks, but Grimvald still felt that he won their bout. He also expected things to go this way eventually anyway.

The king was provided, without his own input, extra meals to 'tide him over' between the main three. It started with a light brunch and a snack between lunch and dinner, but of course by Shiloh's orders those 'snacks' turned into pre-feast sized meals by the end of a few weeks.

Of course Grimvald didn't like it, but he expected it... They only hastened his decline.

Soon King Brock's thighs were always touching as he walked, his arms propped upwards slightly by the size of his chest and the fat of his waist. Between that and every new outfit expansion quickly being outgrown, the king's challenged mobility became increasingly evident. Even the simple action of navigating from his room down the hall to his throne had become an onerous task for him.

But oh, his throne. With his increase in size, the king's behind now overflowed from the generously sized seat. Already crafted twice the size he needed so that he may lounge upon it, now it simply did not accommodate him.

It was short work to remove the arm rests and widen the bench. It took but a few hours and was beautiful handiwork, but it seemed as if the woodworkers underestimated His Majesty's rate of growth. When the king sat upon it,

Grimvald noted that his thighs, spread wide to allow his gut to rest between them, were constricted still by this throne. That was even with his clothes pulling in his true dimensions.

Shaw had also been serving the king more regularly. She provided an elixir for better sleep and various others for the checklist of issues that seemed to pop up like weeds. But, true to her track record, it was child's play for her to solve any issues that came her way.

The issue was what the king called his 'walking staff'.

He was convinced that bed rest for his aches and pains was not necessary, that Shaw's treatments and a hot bath were all he needed to continue as he was.

His exhaustion from simply standing and taking a short trip to another room was seemingly a non-existent issue, or at least was something he refused to talk about with Grimvald.

But the king could definitely not run from his advisor. All he needed to do was wait in the hall for him to pass by in the morning.

The king, seemingly proudly, walked with an unbuttoned shirt, trousers and breeches fully torn at the crotch, and his esquire of the wardrobe, alongside a second member of staff plucked from the halls, both worked together to alleviate some of the king's burden by lifting as much as they could of his drooping gut. His sweat and greasy fur often had them slipping, so on the second day they had set up a hammock of sorts between them.

This is not even to mention the process it took to get the king out of bed in the morning.

He was taking longer and longer to gradually rock back and forth to roll himself to his feet, therefore the staff who walked him to the throne room assisted by pulling him upright. This, of course, took more and more time each morning, which left the king hungrier and hungrier by the time he waddled slowly to the throne room.

He was not fit to walk, Grimvald reminded him. As his feet and even hands began to look fuller, the advisor could only resolve to sending more staff the king's way to form a 'Walking Team' of sorts. He was hoping up until this point that the king could at least get some exercise from walking. That was fully a lost cause now.

He felt as if he had one attempt left in him, a chance to catch the king after a tiring journey back to bed, where he just might be able to talk some sense into him.

So, when the staff departed, the king left only in a breech cloth to sleep in, Grimvald stood by the ajar door. It was exactly open enough that his silhouette fit like a glove. The middling light from the hall made him out a shadow compared to the single dim candle of King Brock's room.

His panting was almost overwhelmingly loud. Grimvald also noted the smell of his sweat as he sat upon his bed, which had been lowered to the floor some weeks earlier.

"Sir, may I speak my mind?" He asked.

The king, unable to produce any words, grunted a confirmation.

"I believe it would benefit you to return to your previous diet, Your Majesty." He didn't want to waste Brock's time by spilling his heart out with worry. It was not in his nature.

After the king had caught his breath, he grumbled out a few words. "Grimvald, it would benefit you to not think of such things as old diets... Now good night."

The king had decided the conversation was over, so Grimvald left without another word. It was simply not his place to push the matter forward. It was his choice after all.

4. Duplicity

There was a small incident during dinner when a massive rip sounded. A tearing of fabric that started with a snap, and did not stop until the king (who did not cease eating) was left unclothed save for the fabric that still clung to his upper arms and strung across his back. Possibly some fabric was still across his crotch and under the fat of his belly, but it was pinned under so much fat that it could not be seen. In fact, this did not disrupt much in hindsight as any shame the king had was simply under too many rolls and layers to be seen.

A solution was suggested by Archibald, actually, who as of late had sported a small waddle of his own. The king could wear outfits that were easier expanded by large cuts of fabric, and fastened to his body in a way that would not need repair as frequently, like buttons. "Like a night gown with a belt at the waist," he explained.

This pleased the king. No longer would he have to wear such restrictive things like trousers or shoes if a robe simply covered all. Archibald was given an entire new carriage and procession of horses to travel to the castle with, though Grimvald would have definitely preferred less time with that snooty bastard around.

But if Brock was happy, so was Grimvald. He did not chide or mope. He simply observed and did all in his power to let the feasts continue.

In private, the two servants of the king did have a small discussion. It seemed that the requirements of the king were changing how food was produced in the kingdom. Rats are not hunters by nature, nor truly carnivorous. Sure, they took small amounts of meat in their diets, enough that farms routinely kept doves to provide fertiliser as well as the occasional added red cuts of meat to a stew, but cows, pigs and the like were rare to keep outside of the big cities where badgers, like the king, lived. As a higher need arose for livestock, the farmers around cities couldn't keep up with Brock's needs, so he alone had caused farmers around Dachstaat to provide what was now an incredibly high-reward food.

This was not a kingdom of capital, not in the least; money was not provided to these farmers so much as rewards like manpower and supply shipments. Money was chiefly used for trade with foreign entities, or gold for crafting beautiful things that could be exchanged for other items of value. That is all to say, eventually you run out of things to offer the farmers as they can only use so many extra hands. Therefore, objects of comfort were being paid out to farms for the first time in Dachstaat's history. He wondered what the inside of these cottages looked like now, outfitted with plush bedding and warm cushy seating.

But that quickly left Grimvald's mind when Archibald left to retire to his office. He had other plush things to think about.

On this morning, before Brock awoke, Grimvald walked

the hall that the king would soon travel down to ensure there was staff at hand in case of emergencies. He made sure Shaw was at the ready with the king's morning medication, and that breakfast would be ready by the time the king arrived at his throne. Which, of course, had been reinforced and widened before the sun rose. Grimvald had grown accustomed now to anticipating what was to come. No longer would any staff or hurdles of King Brock's growing body sneak up on him. He would be ready for anything to come.

Unlike Grimvald, Shiloh had not learned.

She was not done with her petty revenge, and those extra meals grew into an outrageous spread before him each morning, expanding alongside the king.

Even worse was the frequency at which new food arrived. Before, there was an intermission to the feasting. The king and any guests may take an aside to be entertained, given a tour, or, in the case of His Majesty, be escorted to a wet room for a bath or application of salves for his circulation.

But no. Shiloh saw to it that as soon as breakfast concluded a selection of nibbles be set out for the king to snack upon until brunch. Or a sweet treat after lunch to tide him over until dinner – a treat that then led into an array of appetisers. It was getting more and more difficult to pry the king away from his throne. Grimvald would not beg Brock to stand: if the king said no, that was simply the case. So from this day on it seemed it would be simpler to bring the wet room to him.

Grimvald could see where this was going but **chose** to leave that eventuality out of his plans for the time being.

He was foolish to assume that day was so far away.

As he stood at the ready outside of King Brock's bedroom, Grimvald tapped his foot impatiently. He had witnessed the morning crew enter the king's bedroom, and by now Brock should be dressed and standing. But the door remained shut before him, and Grimvald's fear quickly turned to worry, as thoughts of what could be occurring flashed into his mind. But he dismissed them, realising that it did no good to sit and ponder. He decided then to take a breath, prepared for the worst and entered the king's chambers.

The moment Grimvald laid his eyes upon the king he could breathe easily once more. The king was fine... but...

He was sat at the side of his bed, having been clothed sitting down. The four belts that fastened his robe and hoisted his gut closer to his body were being consumed by a shelf of fat above and to the sides. The rolls under his arms and breasts were pushed upwards enough that his arms were permanently angled 60 degrees out from an average person's resting position. The king could not touch the bed below him without angling his entire body to one side, at the risk of lying on the bed once more. With the added weight of his rear, that now covered the majority of the bed's edge, and legs that could barely bend on their own accord let alone lift himself easily... Brock could not stand. Even with the help of three staff.

"Grimvald, sir!" One of the staff, a strong fellow previously from the guard force, spoke up upon the advisor's entrance. He was standing by the king's side, a rat of considerable stature and strength was even dwarfed by the monarch's titanic thigh.

"Next time, call upon me. What is the issue, fatigue?" Staying objective and seeing how the king panted so furiously he could not speak, he thought to resolve this swiftly.

"No sir, His Majesty was feeling well rested. I'm afraid standing is coming with difficulty, sir," the staff member replied.

Nodding, Grimvald called in another pair of strong individuals and organised them in such a way that enough force was positioned to support the king's back as to avoid dislocating anything. By the time they were ready, Brock saved his breath and nodded to confirm his readiness for another attempt.

After rocking back and forth and gathering momentum, on Grimvald's mark the five rats pushed and pulled King Hagan Brock until he had no choice but to stand upon his two feet. But obviously it was not so simple. When the king reached a standing position, his paws stomped in such a way that rattled and shook any unsecured object upon their perches. His momentum continued to a second, then third step at such a speed that Grimvald could not reasonably react fast enough, even if he was sparing a single thought for himself.

He found himself struck by the bulky, pillowy expanse of the king's belly, his entire face enveloped for little more than a second before he fell backwards onto the cold, hard stone floor below. A warmth at the back of his head spread, and a coat of sweat slathered over his snout.

Before Grimvald fell unconscious, he could hear Brock cursing the staff and commanding them to find and bring a healer.

Once Grimvald was taken out of the room to be cared for, the king, who was leaning against one of the dressers, muttered about how inconvenient this all was before waving a hand in the general direction of his walking crew. What was once a simple pair was now a group of five, and even with all of them supporting him Brock could barely take the first step.

He was a proud badger; his whole family line was known for their pride in the face of total failure. It's what had gotten them **this** far. But while he was no quitter, he was only mortal. Though a life of fighting may have brought him strength, it was not at the level of a deity.

But he did not quit, no. He had never quit before, and defeat was the only taste he swore not to savour.

So Brock took his first step. It was laboured. Three of the strongest rats in the building lifted his gut up and forward somewhat. Without the belts he'd been wearing, the fat of his stomach reached lower than his knees, almost to his mid-shin. They obstructed his legs and limited his movement to a shuffle. With those three assisting him his waddle was pronounced but industrious. Yet it was still a waddle, and with each step he threatened to topple over.

This is where the final two assistants act. One for each leg they pushed and called guidance to the three at the front, turning a half inch step into something closer to two or four inches. But that was dependant on how much energy the king had of course. At first it was not a lot. Grimvald's fall dampened his mood. Once the king had progressed a quarter of the way though, a runner arrived from the infirmary to inform the king that his advisor had simply passed out from a mixture of shock and a sudden change of blood pressure. This made enough sense to the king and he focused his distracted mind enough that he picked up the pace, swaying, grunting, panting and at times swearing his way to the throne room on his pained legs.

Upon arrival he was so exhausted that he practically collapsed onto his throne – an act which predictably caused the throne to let out a nasty crack and a groan. It didn't collapse under him (thankfully), but it did bend ever so slightly.

The runner, who was still at the king's side, took post where Grimvald would usually stand in the morning, as if to show to the king that he would convey messages to the infirmary when needed. But Brock's muzzle curled. 'How annoying,' he thought to himself.

"Off with you." He waved his paw a bit fiercer than necessary, frightening the runner, who dashed off quickly.

As mead was poured into his cup, he spoke to the servant who poured it. It didn't outright shock the poor woman, but she did flinch at the thought that she had somehow angered the king. "Speak to whomever is caring for Grimvald. He is to rest; I am not in need of his services today... Is that understood?"

The servant nodded, put the jug of mead down within reach of the king and scurried off to carry out his request.

It couldn't be **that** hard to go one day without Grimvald. The king assured himself silently as he stuffed a butterie into his maw.

As he ate, the poltergeist of Grimvald's hard work moved the world around him. His morning medicines were administered by Shaw, who provided small doses of thick liquid in shot-sized glasses for pain, blood flow, indigestion and to balance his humours. A second individual applied a balm to parts of his skin that chafed and inflamed. He was having difficulty reaching all he hungered for at the table on account of his restricted arms, so a third staff member was present to shift plates into his reach.

A fourth stood by to run requests to the kitchen, in case

the king hungered for something specific during his next meal. But that was standard since day one of the feast.

About halfway into his breakfast the cracking of egg shells could be heard. Two servants peeled hard-boiled eggs for the king as he chowed down on a juicy sausage. Just as he took a massive chomp, the door to his left opened and Archibald wandered into the room, his nose deep in a roll of paper and a runner holding a second just a step behind him. When he came to his destination and stopped. He looked up to speak to Grimvald, who, of course, was not there. So he cut himself off mid-syllable, bowed to the king, and reported to stand in front of His Majesty.

The noble-born rat had similar proportions to how Brock had looked some months ago: a hanging gut, an additional chin, and ample chest. But his multiple layers of clothing attempted to hide this somewhat. They failed to, but the attempt was there.

Archibald cleared his throat, rolling the papers tighter once he had finished scanning over them. When he spoke his nerves were obvious, but he kept a brave enough face to proclaim his point at a decent volume without any sudden squeaks. "Your Majesty." He made sure to stress his respect when he began. "It has come to my attention that the castle is just barely receiving the needed provisions to continue at your... astounding pace. As to not risk the meals falling short of your **powerful** hunger, I come now to ask of your wisdom. What shall be done to secure the meat you require?" He put his hands behind his back, a bead of sweat becoming visible when Brock did something quite out of character.

He put down the link of sausages he was eating, wiped his greasy paws upon his robe (leaving twin trails of deep dark smears) and cleared his throat loud enough to cut through the noise of cracking eggs. The servants paused, allowing the king the silence to be heard clearly.

He took a serious tone, a slight growl at being interrupted. “Archibald, you will send out a missive to each and every colony, town, and village. You will contact our allies to the South. They shall produce what I want as thanks for **my** good will. They **will** send it to be butchered by common folk in the capital. This is **not** instead of any other produce, but in **addition** to. Start at an extra 5% by weight. It can be increased gradually, they’ll barely notice. A second missive will be sent to the unemployed and the butchers of the capital. The unemployed shall become the butchers. The butchers will spend their weekends training them. Be sure to offer a suitable bounty for every head trained this way... Is that **all**?”

Archibald, slightly taken aback, composed himself once more, ensure he had memorised the king’s order, then remembered the runner to his back. He snatched the papers the runner had grasped in their paws and quickly scanned its contents.

“I, um. Hm.” This was not good. Archibald’s forehead grew slick from sweat at this news.

“...Spit it out Archibald,” Growled the king, tapping his claws arrhythmically against the table before him.

“We have news from the Northern outskirts. Some soldiers, or, well, veterans of the previous era, have taken up arms against common folk. Their motives are unknown.” His hands shook almost imperceptibly as he crumpled the paper in both fists.

“Have general Kellshome organise a taskforce and have them **killed!**” Brock slammed his fist against the table, so hard that an egg fell to the ground with a dull splat. “That was an **obvious** choice, Archibald, do not bother me with such trivial tripe ever again."

With that, Archibald bowed deeply, thanked the king at least three times, and left through the main doors with the runner almost stuck to his ankles.

Brock groaned out a sigh as he stuck a sausage into his maw with a freshly peeled egg as a chaser.

The day went by as expected: Brock feasted, refused to leave the comfort of his long-suffering throne, and begrudgingly answered the questions pointed his way.

He was asked what honoured guests this year's Turning of the Seasons festivities should see invited to the castle. He was asked what colour he would like his new cape to be from a selection of three identical reds. He was shown architects' sketches of a new cathedral to be constructed in his honour, which he predictably shoved aside with a wave of a hand to approve.

It was tiring work between all of those interruptions and his own feasting. He had no idea how Grimvald could do it. It almost ruined his appetite!

When the night approached, a selection of cakes lay before the king in an assortment of colours, shapes, and sizes. But he merely picked at them, the hour catching up to him.

That was until the doors behind him open. He didn't turn his head, as he was sure he would be disappointed by yet another trivial matter needing his attention.

"Sir."

"Grimvald!" The king perked up right away, his neck bunching up between his chin and shoulder when he tried to turn his head to see his beloved advisor approach.

He looked healthy: gaze even, posture sturdy, and a small crack of a smile forming at the king's joy.

"You would not believe the day I had, Grimvald!" He kept his sight on the other, the chair below him creaking as he shifted even slightly where he sat. With his stomach so taut and pronounced, every slight movement caused some shift of the table before him or the worrying groan of the throne underneath. With his belts discarded around lunch-time, his gut was free to hang low between his legs, parted as wide as he could comfortably handle.

"I had all sorts of unsavoury characters requesting all types of rubbish of me. Of curtains and silly festivities." He waved a paw dismissively, letting out a shallow belch before knocking his chest to loosen another.

"Is that so?" As Grimvald arrived at his correct position to address him properly, the king tried to shift himself where he sat, his heavy stomach feeling uncomfortable balanced upon its perch.

When he stretched his legs that little more, his heavy thighs loosened from where they were propped up upon his bench. This sudden drop caused his whole body to quiver. The only part of him that settled quickly was his gut, the lowest hanging part landing upon the floor below him. It was firmly resting in fact.

This, of course, distracted Brock, causing him to laugh in an uproar. "Look at that, Grim!" He grabbed the sides of his gut, and gave it a hearty wobble, the furthest of it upon the floor shook only slightly, gliding side to side upon slick wet fur.

Grimvald, perplexed, knelt and lifted the tablecloth. Upon seeing this, he covered his face until he regained his composure. "I-I see." He stood once he was sure he could stay professional.

"Well... Sir. I wanted to make sure you get back to your room without issue before I depart to bed. Additionally, if there are a-"

"Ha! No, Grimvald, everything is handled." He ceased

playing with his own fat and patted what he could reach of his belly. "Every single silly request is squared away, I even had some runt complain, handing me my plates! He shut up quickly upon threat of being **sat upon**!!" Brock thought that was hilarious, so Grimvald smiled and faked a chuckle. It was a scary prospect, but an empty threat. It's not like the king could stand so abruptly... or at all, by the looks of him.

Considering what weight had obviously been added today, Grimvald was doubting the five walking staff would be appropriate. He unfortunately had a suggestion to make in this situation.

"Sire. May I please make a suggestion?" Grimvald took a seat across from the king, shifting it to sit as if they were dining together.

The king's laughter subsided. He kept a light tone as he nodded and motioned for Grimvald to speak freely.

"May I move your bedding and install curtains **here** in the throne room? I fear that walking has grown... unsafe... as of late. If not for me, for you, sire. I worry that if the staff were to lead you astray or fail in their duties walking with you, you may not be able to stand as easily in the hall. Or you may even get injured yourself." When he thought to stop talking, Grimvald found himself rambling on about his fears. He saw a look on Brock's face he hadn't seen before. Perhaps it was an **empathetic** wide-eyed stare? He hoped so at least.

"Well," Brock started, slapping what little he could reach of his thighs over the sides of his gut. "I cannot deny how unwieldy the trip into the throne room is. At least tonight I'm much too tired to make such a trip!" He grinned, his sharp teeth looking keen. "Have the staff bring plenty of creature comforts, and incense from the chapel for the smell, lest I stay awake all night thinking of my previous meal." The king loosened another hearty laugh. Relieved, Grimvald breathed easy but immediately gasped at the sound of Brock's bench breaking beneath his titanic rear.

Thankfully Brock found the whole situation equally as hilarious as the spectre of dinners past haunting him.

Grimvald headed the first half hour of setting up the king's 'temporary' sleeping quarters, as well as the removal of the broken bench. The plans for the next iteration were set into motion before he departed.

On his way to his tower, Grimvald spotted Shaw waiting outside of the king's quarters with an assortment of bottles and pouches in her arms.

At first, in the mood he was in, he thought to simply point her in Brock's direction. But he quickly realised something.

"What **is** all of that, Shaw?" Grimvald asked pointedly, gesturing to the strange collection she held.

"Oh! Ha, yes, this is to help him sleep." She jiggled a bottle of milky white liquid. "This is for his breathing." She gestured to a bundle of assorted sprigs and leaves. "This is to help him digest more efficiently," as she pointed to a black tonic. Grimvald went ahead and grabbed it.

"It what?" He scanned the strange liquid without risking opening the bottle.

"I, um, it makes it so that he can digest food faster, y'know... so he gets bigger like he wants... I thought you knew that..." She backed off a step, looking sheepish.

It seemed so. It did look like that's what the king wanted. Grimvald stood stock still, wordless, his ears going red.

"...Shiloh assured me you ordered the dosage to be upped." Shaw finished, truly looking scared when Grimvald's head whipped up, eyes wide with rage.

"She WHAT!?"

5. Crushed

He would get his revenge. Oh yes, he would. If Shiloh wanted to play this game, then who was he to deny such a challenge? Had she forgotten that he had lived the majority of his life in the uncaring caress of combat? That he was practically raised with a map in his paws, the king at his side, and arrows flying overhead?

She stood no chance living so peacefully in his castle. She thought she knew heat. Ha! Soon she will be begging to be stuffed into the oven, after he introduced her to the fires of hell.

Grimvald was going to **crush** her under his heel.

But he was also a busy man.

He could do oh so many things right now. Throw any number of festivals to be catered, have her personally run around to organise a re-fitting of the throne room. He could have a tailor strategically cut stitches in her gowns and shoes to frazzle her, slowly driving her naked and insane.

But patience is a virtue for a reason. He would find his moment to strike, and it will only be more glorious for the anticipation.

No need to rush for the sake of a child's prank.

As the day of Brock sleeping in the throne room turned to a week, the monarch made a number of requests. For one, a curtain partition, so he may seclude himself into a smaller, more private space as he slept. Over time more and more pillows were called in, large blankets and downy duvets were turned into a kind of mat for him to sleep upon. This created a nest of sorts where Brock would lounge, surrounded by tables cut down to a height that kept his meals at eye level from his new position on the floor.

With his new lifestyle, he even found that his beloved robes did not serve their purpose well as he spent so much time lying around, and, upon coming to the realisation that he could bend societal taboo to his will, cast aside the notion of being fully clothed. Instead, the king simply wore a cape, and upon Grimvald's request, a tabard of sorts upon his front. This tabard was fastened in place by what must've been at least five belts. But as they disappeared under the king's bulk most of the time, Grimvald really couldn't be sure.

As unbelievable as the notion may be, the king did still stand and walk from time to time.

The trips were short, and usually he only stood (assisted by several rats, of course) to readjust himself or to use a chamber pot. But predictably, this era did not last very long.

It was no secret that walking to and from his quarters to wherever he wished to dine was his only source of exercise. With that lost, the king's weight gain once again increased in momentum. Within the month a day did come when even though he was assisted by a dozen rats, the king attempted once, then twice, to stand, only to drop back onto his rear. This of course caused Grimvald to be called away from a meeting with an ambassador to discuss the matter.

"Well, sir, we tried everything we could," said a scrawny link, fur tousled and eyes darting about as if he was staring at the face of death.

Grimvald supposed he could lift his scowl some – his expression was known to scare the younger pups in the castle. He tried to give a smile, but it came across as insincere with how his expression quickly shifted back into a frown.

"And His Majesty is refusing to continue trying?" Grimvald asked.

"Yes, sir. He sounded mighty frustrated at first, but took to laughing and drinking soon afterwards."

The advisor mumbled out a barely audible "I see," before nodding to himself and looking towards the room he'd been taking a meeting in just a few minutes before.

"Keep the king entertained for another half an hour, I shall be there as soon as possible."

The link bowed and scurried off back towards the throne room, leaving Grimvald to pick up the pieces.

He'd have to wrap up the meeting quickly enough that he did not offend his guest, while also returning to Brock's side before the king grew frustrated with Grimvald's absence upon request.

He sighed, cleared his throat, corrected his posture and returned to his meeting.

The ambassador, a bird-like fellow representing the Tringu nation, stood with a translator by his side, both in traditional toga adorned with complex stitching and beaded hems. Their heads resembled fowl, with long golden brown and iridescent green feathers upon the crown.

The translator acknowledged Grimvald's entrance immediately, while the ambassador continued to admire a shelf of shining baubles and curios. The room was made for purpose, to show just enough humility with the small size of the space, while also hinting at the greater wealth beyond if these wonders are what they had on display in such a reserved space.

Grimvald bowed his head as he shut the door behind himself, apologising for the interruption, only to raise it to see both of the Tringites squabbling with one-another.

Well. It occurred to him in that moment he was unsure of who to look at when he spoke now. They could've been twins: identical clothing, similarly sized plumes of feathers, the same golden browns and greens. The fact that he didn't notice who spoke first and who spoke last made this more difficult than it had to be.

"Erm. Well." He chose left. "It was an honour meeting you, bu-"

"Hrrk!" The one on the right made a sound like a chicken being shot from a cannon, then babbled a frustrated sentence out to his interpreter on the left who said:

"He is tired of being pushed about between staff members! Kaffloh represents the ruling queen of Tringu and deserves to parlay with King Brock himself!" The rage was obvious from both strangled voices. The interruption followed by such offence was a step too far.

Grimvald was sure they did not know what they were really asking for, and gave ambassador Kaffloh an opportunity to spare himself from the king's wrath. "Sir, I meant no offence. His Majesty is predisposed. Your interfacing with him will reflect badly upon your kingdom if he is displeased. I'm sure you wish only the best for the people of Tringu."

The translator could only get halfway through repeating Grimvald's plea to the ambassador before a second awful noise escaped his throat, and he demanded his opinion known: "This will happen now," said the interpreter.

After holding back a scoff, Grimvald relented. Who was he to prevent the inevitability of a fool acting foolishly?

He had done all he could.

As politely as he could, he led the pair out of their little meeting room and down the hall. They passed a number of confused servants who dared not question Grimvald's actions. Then, as they drew closer, they passed a pair of guards, who had looks resembling those who watch their close relations be sent into a fighting pit, a concern held back only by the hope that someone knew what they were doing.

At the grand oak doors the advisor paused. Turning sharply to face the foreign guests, he gave a final piece of advice. "I know you are of a sound mind to know how to properly address the king, but I must warn you that he is currently feasting, and is not guaranteed to break at your arrival. I would suggest-"

"Hm! Yes, yes. We know. I must speak to the king now." The ambassador waved a clawed hand as if to shoo away the rat standing between him and the king. This was a manoeuvrer that caused Grimvald to fully withdraw any plans to placate the king when this inevitably went south.

So, Grimvald straightened his posture, cleared his throat and opened the doors, a pair of servants at the other side quickly moved to assist, allowing a smooth and quiet swing of the doors, opening to reveal the scene before them.

The tables, with legs cut short to allow the king easy access to the bounty atop them, were overflowing with decadent cakes, sugar-dusted mince pies, fruits and berries swimming in cream and an array of cookies, some flavoured with dried currents and others with foreign delicacies like ground dried beans and spicy bark.

This was the king's first dessert of the day, the one that

followed his lunch. Not to be mistaken, of course, with his post-breakfast sweet or his pre-dinner snack.

The king could only be partially seen behind this barricade, but fully heard. He seemingly had not noticed the doors to the throne room were open, and at this moment was shoving a large sponge cake slathered in clotted cream and berry jam into his maw. It was soft and moist enough that he barely needed to chew, so the sound of him licking his sticky paws filled the room as he made little pleasured rumbles at the tasty treats.

What **could** be seen caused both Tringites to baulk.

Under the table the king's lower half lounged lazily upon once beautiful silks and embroidered pillows, now stained by gravy and grease from the previous meal. His legs, engorged, splayed and flattened out at the thigh to such a degree that he likely could not reach out and touch the widest points of his body. Even if he could, his feet were losing a battle with his ankle fat, the soft skin now irritated from contact with the floor while walking.

His gut was a marvel in its own right, so large and heavy that it parted his equally engorged legs to each side of it as it took all the space it could conquer in front of the monarch. It enveloped the space under the main dining table that the king was eating from, and as he ate, guzzling down cakes with unwavering ferocity, it could almost be seen pushing further and further. It was beginning to graze the table legs in such a way that it might push Brock's meal away from him. Those in attendance were transfixed by the sight, but hoped that it was simply the king slowly leaning further and further forwards.

Grimvald noted this, his eye twitching at this new, strange occurrence.

Without any semblance of awareness, the ambassador

spoke, and after a moment of fear, the interpreter translated:

"Greetings Your Highness, King Hagan Brock of glorious Dachstaat! I am the Tringu ambassador, Kaffloh. I have come to discuss the trade deal between our two nations on behalf of my queen. She is under the impression that the Dachstaat ambassador received incorrect information, and upon receiving supply orders that matched the aforementioned 'mistake' has kindly refrained from receiving the requested timber and marble."

As Kaffloh continued, the king moved from the now destroyed cake onto a plate of cookies, crunching them loudly. It somehow did not drown out either voice.

"Therefore, Your Majesty, all members of the Tringu council agree that new terms shall be agreed upon here in your court, with myself as absolute witness. If you agree to this, I'm sure you will find it obvious that the numbers requested of us are obviously the result of a clerical error.

I quote, sir, 250 tons of sugarcane, honey, and beet sugar. Surely Dachstaat does not request a cargo ship's worth of sugar? Another, 10,000 domestic swine by the end of the year! Your Highness, I fully understand that this is not a mistake of yours, but the soldiers sent to collect alongside the requested building materials incorrectly assure us of the paperwork being in order!

"If you could simply confirm a mistake has been made, we shall be on our way and... hm. You may continue to enjoy your... wonderful feast."

Only when Kaffloh stopped and took a backwards step did the king stop eating.

Both of them swallowed heavily.

The king grumbled a growl before speaking, his booming voice causing all but Grimvald to flinch. "Well, finally the bird's done chattering!" Brock slammed his fist against one of the few empty spots atop the table, causing a terrible thud and a clatter as dishes jumped on the spot.

"What made your queen think that Tringu had a **choice** in this trade!? Was it the armed armada or the messenger who refused to take **no** for an answer? You're a joke! I should have bells sewn to your ridiculous outfit!" With an escalation of volume reaching a boiling point, the sudden pause in the king's rant would have usually caused envoys to piss themselves. They must have felt safe in the thought that the king could not personally grab them by the necks from this far away.

That was until the king continued.

"I'm tired of them! Have them parboiled, plucked, and then **roasted upon a spit!!**"

The translator loosened a strained squawk as he fainted on the spot, leaving Kaffloh trembling and mumbling in his native tongue. While his interpreter was unable to tell him what the king had just said, he was sure he knew what was happening by the way the guards and servants were all looking at him.

Grimvald sighed, then drifted to the interpreter and gave him a heavy shove with his foot. The avian snapped awake and slapped his hands over his beak to stop himself from screaming.

The king, seemingly unaware that they were still present, had resumed eating at this point. The sound overwhelmed the panic of the two Tringites, so when the guards took both of them under their custody Grimvald spoke to the now mostly conscious bird. "Tell your boss that you must leave immediately under threat of death. If the trade is not honoured, the Queen will have more to worry about than sugar and pigs."

After spitting those last words, he turned his attention to the guards.

"The king was exaggerating. Escort them back to their carriage and onwards to the shore. See that they do not dawdle or stray... If they do? They shall be escorted back here and enter through the pantry."

With that, orders were followed and the room was emptied at Grimvald's request, leaving only him and the king to have—or rather, attempt—a private discussion.

Brock wasn't finished with his desserts, so as Grimvald stood prim and proper before him it was as if he did not exist.

He did not blame Brock, not really. The king rarely acknowledged his advisor as he ate. It was as much a part of their routine as poking fun at entertainers together, but Grimvald was not in the mood for japes. Quite the opposite; his frustration was mounting, and without relief madness would surely consume him.

"Your Highness," he said, trying to speak during a relatively quiet moment.

Of course, he did nothing but continue, offering a small grunt. It was hard to tell what it was in response to.

"Brock." With emphasis and volume that kicked the air, the king involuntarily twitched an ear at the interruption.

With a louder grunt the monarch sat back slightly, raising his head. His brows furrowed. He was not ready to stop. Brock wiped his hands together ineffectively and shifted a little under 20 degrees to half-heartedly face his advisor.

"Yes," he spoke bitterly, "Grimvald?"

"Is your goal to create enemies of every king, queen, noble and peasant? Or is that simply an oversight in some grander scheme? Dachstaat has never been so lowly as to shortchange even an unwilling trade. Why now, in times of peace?" He wasn't making eye contact with his king, he didn't deserve it in this moment. He was not some god who could toy with the world as he pleased, he was a greedy, stubborn mortal like the rest of the pitiful people of this country.

He held his silence, simply placing his paws upon his exposed thighs, his teeth gripping nothing but themselves with an audible creak.

"And you speak of consuming **guests** upon your land. Not even the most deranged of landlords would threaten such a thing. You **sit** there, unmoving, **UNABLE** to move, while your people toil to serve you, and despite their unwavering loyalty to you, you **threaten** their very lives by moving on the world stage as a stumbling **bully**.

"You're a fucking disgrace to the King I used to respect!" With that, Grimvald swiped the air with his hand, his cape fluttering, the only minute noise in the dead silence that fell upon the throne room.

When Brock, who was seething quietly, suddenly lunged forwards, Grimvald was caught unawares. The tables were cast astride by the manoeuvrer, platters clattering and liquid splashing from pitchers and pie fillings as the comparatively miniature rat was pinned under his king, only his head remaining exposed from under Brock's bulk.

The position would have spared him suffocation if it wasn't for the unrestrained weight upon him, turning any breath into a pathetic shudder. He found no purchase to struggle loose, either. The badger's body was so slick with sweat that he simply could not wriggle free.

Brock panted heavily. Between the sickly sweet smell of his breath and his overpowering musk, Grimvald found his mouth paralysed. They both lay there in silence for who knows how long, with Grimvald getting gradually more and more lightheaded from the lack of oxygen.

Eventually Brock spoke. Grimvald could hear his deep, booming voice rumbling through the entirety of their bodies.

"As much as I respect your honesty before me, **Grimvald**, it is disappointing that I must once again make this clear after so much good work from you."

Grimvald's vision started to blur. A great abstract field of black, grey and white formed before his eyes as the king continued.

"Whatever qualms you have with my choices **must** be discarded. If I wish to **eat,** I shall **eat.** It does not matter how much, when, or **who**. As king, I am god's will incarnate, so if I wish to eat until I *fill this entire room,* then my will shall be **DONE.** Is that clear enough for you?" With a final snarl, the king's massive arms, furled by the muscle of a warrior and the adrenaline of power, lifted his upper torso up and off of the rat. Even so, Brock's massive, soft chest still graced Grimvald's body, ghosting over the majority of his torso.

After a bout of laboured breathing and the realisation that he had suffered at least one broken rib, he spoke. "Yes, sir, crystal."

Heaving to his side with a grunt of exhaustion, the king finally freed his advisor. It took some time to right himself, several minutes more to shuffle back to his 'throne'. As if nothing had happened, Brock retrieved a platter of cookies from a table that had not been knocked aside and continued eating. Grimvald was left to recover upon the floor, damp from sweat and stiff from the pain. While he was not able to fully collect himself, Grimvald's powers of damage control were to be envied, as he was able to return to his quarters with only minimal suspicion that something odd had occurred.

He did not return to the throne room that day. Shaw was called to assist with his 'horse riding injury', and couriers were sent to order Shiloh about to keep her too busy to notice any anomalies.

But that night, as the servants finally retired to their quarters, as Brock slept, and as Grimvald nursed his wounds by candlelight, he couldn't help but hold his sweat-drenched doublet in both paws to remind himself of the small moment in which it hadn't hurt.

Part 2

6. The Turning of the Seasons

What a joyous time to be a citizen of Dachstaat!

The king's wisdom had created many fruitful opportunities for the people. Farmers lived like those of the city, in comfort and wealth. The butchers were like noblemen, paid to be scholars, invited to create factotum for their students. Even the sailors, couriers and cannoneers of the cargo lines saw wealth as many more shipping routes opened into the heart of once-unapproachable foreign lands. Dachstaat had not forgotten the vice-like grip she had on other nations, and it seemed neither had they.

As time passed, more and more emissaries were sent out to Dachstaat to offer their ports as lively trade hubs so that they may work with the prosperous nation.

Adler had, of course, seen success too in this new regime. It was from his looms that the king's personal tailors purchased cloth. Adler, and by extension the entire Whiskerstitch family, saw great success for the first few months of this new era. Why, it had seemed as if the castle had ordered new clothing for their each and every staff member,

as well as a new wardrobe for His Majesty.

But now, orders had all dried up! He wasn't complaining (not out loud at least), but he so rarely received inquiries or requests for samples...

This is why he was so enthused to receive an invitation from the castle. He was to attend the Turning of the Seasons festival, a wonderful affair where, as winter finally turned to spring, all who gathered would compete in jolly games, sing the ballads of the first flowers and take part in a feast of the most exceptional delicacies from around the country.

To have but a taste of the castle's cooking, it would make the entire event worthwhile, and maybe, oh, maybe he'd be able to get a word in with one of the tailors.

Adler went to rifle through his wardrobe, pulling out several suitable outfits for a day of sport and garden lunching before he spied a line of text at the bottom of his invitation.

'This year the festival will be hosted exclusively **inside** of Castle Hordrigg.'

"How odd," Adler Whiskerstitch thought to himself a moment before switching out his outfits for more **refined** options.

The outdoor décor was as he remembered when he arrived upon horseback. The ride up the hill was lined with garlands, finely-cut hedges, paper flowers and colourful bunting.

Through the open gate, past the grand stone outer walls, and into the throng of the crowds, the smell of wine was in the air already, and cheers sounded when old friends arrived as if they had freshly emerged from hibernation to relieve a long loneliness.

Adler was greeted by welcomes and warm embraces

aplenty. It felt like homecoming.

While there was chatter about how odd having the celebration indoors would be, it was, as always, a cold enough day that nobody complained when they were escorted inside the castle proper.

How wonderful it was inside. Sconces burned brightly, warming the body. The smells of baking bread reached every guest even from the far-away kitchens. The march up the long flight of stairs to the feasting chamber was made in good spirits, but those at the head of the crowd let out sounds of confusion loud enough that Adler could hear them all the way at the back.

He didn't learn why until later. All of them were led not to the main hall, but to the king's throne room. He assumed for an address, a speech.

Naturally he was one of the last to enter the room, one of the last in fact to be seated. By the looks of it they would be kicking off celebrations by drinking. That was odd, but, well, who was he to complain?

Indeed, a jovial tone was taken in the room as the guests poured wine for each other and politely refrained from drinking until each and every person had a full cup in their paws.

As this went underway Adler was doing little more than grinning at the smell of the drink under his nose, so he took a moment to appreciate the king's throne room.

Great iron wrought chandeliers lit the space, illuminating white marble tiled flooring, massive oak tables arranged in a 'U' where his comrades sat and chatted, dark stone walls that surrounded them and... A massive curtain.

Adler had only now noticed the king was nowhere to be found and where the throne usually sat was an outrageously large floor to ceiling curtain created using **his** fabric! Adler was honoured, obviously, so much so that he did not question a single thing when entertainment was brought forth to play an arrangement in the centre of the tables. At which point all gathered began to drink.

The festivities went on for several minutes, but like with the opening bars of the orchestra in the pit, eventually the curtain had to open and the star of the show was to be revealed.

When servants moved to the far left and right of the throne room to pull open the curtain, Adler, and in fact all gathered, stood to properly greet their king.

Some raised their glasses, some bowed, some applauded.

All faltered when they saw the badger before them.

The king was unlike any person they had seen before. In fact, some guests took embarrassingly long to even realise that the shape before them **was** a person. Where he sat upon a spread of blankets, padded mats, pillows and furs, the king had no chair to support him save the facade of a throne's back bolted into the stone. All present would agree that there was no chair in the kingdom that could support his bulk.

What was visible of the king was primarily his stomach, engorged from a breakfast so large that he had fallen asleep after. There was a partially noticeable roundness to the highest point of his gut which rivalled the size of his entire midsection during his last public outing at the joust. Now that was just a low peak of the mountain; the rest, gelatinous from the small movements he made, flowed outwards from his body, resting on the floor several feet in front of him.

He of course wore the **finest** crimson fabrics, beautifully lined with golden thread and all worn like a tabard. It extended from his lowest chin to a foot below his navel.

At the shoulders two golden hoops fastened the tabard to a dark cape which draped down his back and covered almost everything that was unseen from the front.

His legs, the only part of his body that attempted to interrupt the all-consuming nature of his gut, were no longer fit to be described as legs at all. They were more suited now to the task of storage for more fat deposits. Only his toes had any chance of movement. At the hip his legs were so splayed to the sides that they could not budge in or out any more. At the knee, his legs were padded in such a way that there was no hope of bending, and at the ankle the fat of his foot had started to consume the appendage.

To speak of the parts of his body that could move, his heaving chest laid heavily upon his gut, but moved vigorously when he raised a paw with a goblet of wine in his thick-fingered grip.

At this point, with his considerable strength, lifting his entire arm was done with practised grace, but his arms in total must have weighed something equal to five rats, **each!** As he did so, his upper arm hung enough that it still stuck to his overflowing sides. He smiled at all present, his wobbling cheeks and chins creasing to accommodate the shift.

But his smile began to fade. His loyal subjects stood gawking like lambs at the slaughterhouse. What had possessed them? Just as King Brock was beginning to feel the first pangs of rage rise to light did Grimvald, ever so dutifully at his side, raise his paws to clap sharply two times and raise his voice to address all present:

"Let us make a toast to His Highness, King Hagan Brock the Mighty Crushing Paw, in thanks for inviting us all to his Turning of the Seasons celebration!"

As if remembering their manners, each member of nobility present took up their cups and called out: "Long live the King!" before taking a deep, deep drink and cheering forth towards him.

Brock spoke under his breath to Grimvald, "They were stunned into silence by the grand reveal, yes?"

"Yes, my liege." Grimvald replied. "Any mortal would be at the sight of your grandiose achievement." Of course it was an achievement. How could anyone have referred to his work in any other terms until now? When nobles grew soft from riches, nobody would think twice. That was a signifier of success, of course. Nobody here was dull enough to not make that connection with the king, and he knew that. His size put all attending in their places as lesser.

Despite his pride the king kept a straight face, so neither at the head of the table showed emotion when they spoke. When Adler looked at the king and his advisor from where he stood, he had no clue where the king's true temperament stood.

It was no matter to him. He was shocked, yes. This was unheard of, thought to be impossible; at least, no rat had reached such a form... Maybe there was some stock in a king's will being that of a god. Or all in the room were suffering a shared delusion.

Whichever option was the case, it did not change the fact that food was arriving – which was odd, but now that he'd seen the king, not a mystery.

The servants, with lightning speed, served whole glazed ducks, platters of grilled pork on beds of shredded leafy greens, bread rolls and sauce soaked shredded beef. All was served first to the king, dish after dish brought in front of him. He obviously could not reach the table from where he sat, but all were witness to another reveal.

Above the king a series of rails, pulleys, ropes and new, never seen mechanisms lowered a polished surface before

His Majesty. A number of staff quickly pushed plates from the main table to the floating one using specialised poles that looked like man-catchers. Not at random, no. The king would simply begin to move his hand toward a plate and by the time it was outstretched the dish was pushed into reach.

Similarly for his drink, as no rat could reach his hand to refill the king's wine, specialised poles with jugs affixed poured more drink when he was not looking.

He of course ate with his bare hands, tearing into handfuls with his vicious teeth.

It was all so mesmerising that nobody noticed when they themselves were presented with their own feast. It was a feast of much more modest dishes: roasted vegetables in a rich plum sauce, scotch eggs freshly hot from the oil, thick warming pottage, spiced roasted root vegetables cooked in bacon fat.

It was overwhelming to some, and just the first course!

Those who had eaten breakfast before arriving took the meal slowly, but Adler, who knew what to expect from a royal feast, had saved plenty of space for today and sampled all he could reach.

He knew the speed that dishes would circulate – if a platter no longer looked succulent, beautiful, or bountiful, it was pulled from the table to be given to servants. While that seemed to take place still with some plates, others were pulled aside, gathered together, and bundled into a single serving to be brought to the king.

There was a concerted effort to not let him see this. Obviously he would be offended, so nobody dared say a word. By the amount of food he could put away into his gargantuan gut, it would have been foolish to mark so much that he would otherwise enjoy as waste.

When one of these plates was brought to him, he reacted

with wonder at the variety and quickly began to guzzle the morsels in new combinations.

The meal proceeded like this wordlessly for some time until Brock seemed to slow his pace. The king still ate at a great pace, but his initial hungered frenzy had passed, and he instead paid some attention to his surroundings.

"Nikolash!" His Majesty said, cutting through the noise of clattering cutlery so sharply that a few dozen individuals froze in place. A bolus of partially-chewed bread splattered near a servant's foot.

"Yes, Your Majesty," a rat with a thick wintery accent and similarly pale fur replied, a rough-and-tumble-looking fellow of scars and stub ears. No fear was shaken into him by being picked out of the crowd. Adler knew him as some breed of arms dealer, producing weaponry for the old regime.

"Do you still keep those big lizards? Or have you sought a normal hobby, hm?"

The jab from the king was taken lightly by the rat who gave a stoic chortle before replying, cutlery politely down as Brock continued to eat. "My liege, you'll be glad to know that I keep even stranger beasts now. Savannah unicorns, apes, creatures from every corner."

"Aha! Never one to give in! They'll take your nose next, I swear, Nikolash! I could've sworn they would've by now, if not for the pink on your snout with that stable-stink you've tracked in here, hm!" Brock grinned as a few individuals around Nikolash elbowed his ribs and laughed along with him.

He took the teasing gracefully as he replied. "If you don't ban me for the assault on your nostrils my lord, I promise to bring some exotics as entertainment when you would permit. The castle has plenty of space for a few birds, sir. Some can even master speech!"

"Speech! Birds, really? Talking?" Brock even seemed to slow his pace to listen carefully now.

"Yes, my lord." Nikolash nodded as he continued. "We have a parrot that can recite some amusingly perverse limericks!"

"Looks like we may have to fire the court jester! Birds are the future of entertainment it seems." Half-jokingly the king waved his hand fancifully at the thought, but stopped mid-movement when a new voice chimed in.

"Your Majesty, do keep your excitement at bay. They're no poultry to snack upon!" said Lady Vogt. Adler knew little of her; her business is barrel production. Or possibly **was**. By the silence, many in the room thought this a rude remark toward someone of higher status, but worse of all, such a rude thing to say to a **king**. Grimvald seemed to visibly tense.

But. The king grinned. Lady Vogt, who had every muscle tensed when silence fell, only moved again when the king's head tilted backwards with mad laughter. So she too laughed, and then all else joined in.

King Brock pointed to her with a greasy paw. "Give the good lady another drink and never let her cup become dry!"

As the conversation continued the king's mood shifted to and fro. At one point the musicians were dismissed by Brock throwing a mostly-eaten turkey thigh at them. A magician displayed her tricks for at most half an hour before Brock grew tired of her gimmicks and demanded her show be ended so he may chat with his guests once more.

Now that all present had been drinking and eating into the evening, the conversation moved on in a chaotic fashion. Several different discussions were happening; some spoke of magicians from other countries they had witnessed, some of sexual encounters, others of bandits roving the land. The king spoke of countries he had visited during his campaign. Adler wasn't shy, but he had little to say. It's not that he was boring, but that he enjoyed a good story, so when the king spoke, he did all he could to listen over the dozens of other voices in the hall.

At this moment the king was not eating. It had been several hours of heavy meats and breads, so while nibbles were laid about to satiate everyone while they drank, he did not partake. Brock spoke of jungle warriors wielding venom-drenched weapons, scorching deserts, high mountain temples, and a scattering more little nuggets of interest. But one individual, a general of renown named Konrad, had something else in mind in the way of discovery.

"That's all well and good your highness," Konrad started, leaning sloppily against the table before him. "But you must have plenty of stories of, ha, well, conquests of the flesh, no?"

"Of the flesh!" He laughed in response, "how brave you are to ask for stories of whom I have bedded on foreign soil. What is your goal? To find an illegitimate son to drag before me? Konrad, you cad!"

"No sire, no," Konrad responded with fear at first, but noted soon after that Brock was not offended, as once again he was teasing, so after a delayed laugh he continued. "There is much talk in the kingdom of heirs, yes, of a... Queen, perhaps?" Scant few people could survive out of line like this; one of them was the general. It was widely known that Brock despised others meddling in his romantic life, so much so that talk of marriages and queens was practically outlawed on the grounds of Castle Hordrigg.

Luckily for Konrad, the king was quite drunk and took the prying in stride. "Do you take me for a fool, Konrad?"

He leaned forward some, chest squishing upwards, his gut forming new creases. His voice seemed as if he were whispering, but he spoke at his regular volume with an unhushed growl instead.

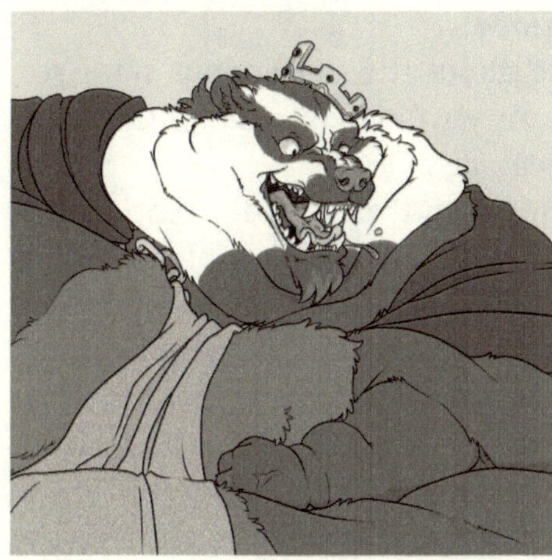

"If I were to take a wife, I'd have to **share** all of this! There is no mortal upon this coil that deserves such an honour as I! Next you'll be showing me portraits and lockets stuffed to the brim with fur, so that you may observe some poor young woman court this old king, you pervert!"

There was a snap to Brock's jaw as he finished, and an iron grip to Konrad's jaw from offence that prevented him from chuckling along to the king's remarks.

Adler observed all of this with laughs on cue and an eye to the faces in the crowd. Most shared his disposition, doing their best to blend into each other as the king's loving audience. But for this entire train of thought, the king's advisor sitting to his right looked, well, antsy, in a word. Then, as he saw Konrad's offence and the king's rising impatience, he seemed to turn outright **agitated**.

"I'm only looking to provide you with a fair maiden to serve you as only a wife can, sir," Konrad said through gritted teeth.

It seemed the king was onto something with what all others gathered clocked as an assumption. All those thinking this fell silent upon the realisation, especially when

Brock leaned forward a few inches more, leaning on his table, causing it to creak loudly.

"And I tell you time and time again, Konrad. Your obsession with this topic is vile." The badger's teeth shone in the low light as a snarl formed.

"I could say the same about the horrendous state you have put yourself in, **sire**. Any woman or man for that matter would turn their noses up at y-"

"Have him apprehended and executed." Not with a shout, a growl, or a huff of frustration. He simply raised his voice to be heard clearly by the guards at the opposite side of the hall. Like a plain and simple matter, he gave a dismissive wave of the hand as he sat back against his throne facade with a goblet taken up by his other paw as he relaxed. An image of boredom, or perhaps a strange disguise.

But it was no matter. Grimvald nodded at the two approaching guards who easily grabbed the general, one arm each. He did not struggle or yell at first, for he was reeling so from surprise that he did not figure out what was going on until he was at the threshold of the throne rooms doors. Then he, of course, yelled out, begged, pleaded, cried, and urinated all the way down the entrance hall's stairs and out into the courtyard, where no guest could hear him anymore.

Brock, like nothing had happened, drank deeply, remarked upon the age of the wine that all in attendance were drinking, then cracked a joke about there being more for him to enjoy now that there was one less guest present.

A joke that all present laughed at much too quickly.

Adler decided not to look into conversing with the castle's tailor.

While the rest of the day proceeded without incident – the ceremonial singing when the sun set, games played indoors, a series of entertainers coming and going during the final courses – Adler could not shake how imposing His Majesty was now. Well, he was imposing before, obviously; such a badger was a sight to behold as a skilled warrior. But as a glutton so fat that he could not stand from where he sat? So fickle as to execute a member of his top brass for talking out of line? He wondered what else such a man could be capable of.

But one thing scared him above all else, so much more than a king the size of Brock, of an execution during a party...

It was the look of satisfaction on his advisor's face when the king made his order, moments after the advisor laid a hand on the king's side. It was the serene smile he gave while everyone else watched General Konrad get dragged off to his death...

He was sure he was imagining things. He had to be.

7. Impatience

There were times when the routine was broken. When visitors came after the feast to further reconnect with the king, when promises made while drunk reared their heads again, when official ceremonies were forced to take place in the throne room.

But otherwise, time went by in a flash. Not because it was boring, no. There was plenty to do, day and night. Messages to relay, entertainment to shuttle, construction to be done.

But oh, the construction.

As the king grew ever larger, so did his needs; among them, the obvious note of waste.

It was unavoidable that someone of such a size would outgrow a chamberpot as even lifting his rear became an impossibility. So instead, one of the basement vaults was repurposed into a septic-room with a chute connecting upwards to the throne room's floor. The system worked surprisingly well, and with how well-reinforced the castle's foundations were, allowed for zero disruption to His Majesty during construction.

While blankets and sheets were laid down during his growth, the fact stood that such simple slings would not suffice in lifting any part of the king's body. The entire lifting staff had difficulty raising only the king's gut with such a method.

So, the rails, ropes and pulleys once only used to better feed the king were expanded outward. This was still in construction, but the plan was that, using chains and fastenings connected to the ceiling, pre-positioned slings could be connected and hoisted upwards by pairs of smaller teams using pulleys.

It wouldn't do forever, but it would have to for as long as it worked.

The other main concern was the king's health.

It was known by any who gazed upon His Highness that such a weight was thought to be impossible. There were many reports of much smaller rats who had perished suddenly clutching their chests or stopped breathing through the night. But through either sheer divine power or luck, the king suffered no major ills or close calls. He definitely wasn't healthy, no. The king's laboured breathing, how his skin showed through thinning fur red and irritated; these worried Grimvald to no end. The king was in great pain. He would never speak of them of course, but it was noticeable when the king was moved too quickly, or in private moments, how he would curl his lip upwards and wrinkle his nose at minor displeasures.

Of course, Grimvald and Shaw were there to treat these ailments. While not much could be done for his breathing, Grimvald knew of ways to increase the quality of the air. There were plenty of foreign aromatics that, when dispersed, would cleanse imperfection and boost the health of those who inhaled it. Seal bile, kelpie gills, volcanic salamander mucus; they were all key ingredients for such aromatic concoctions, and easily procured from those wishing to impress their king.

Shaw of course provided her potions and poultices as usual. In fact, due to her increasing workload, an entire staff was appointed to her. While merely working to recipes, she was rightfully overbearing about the little details, like counting seeds instead of weighing them to ensure that none were broken, or personally checking over leaves to prevent diseased samples from being used.

It worked out like it always did – the poultices would soothe irritated skin and the drugs would mitigate the pain.

Furthermore, his appetite would be augmented through a potion that Grimvald didn't quite understand. Brock had taken it before and continued to do so when his weight gain seemed to be slowing down by his own judgement. It wasn't, it was just less obvious when one couldn't see themselves in the mirror. But the king's say was final as always. For now they could only make him hungrier, but Shaw's staff were diligently working on something to make His Highness happier with his rate of growth.

But the final thing to address when caring for such a large badger was cleanliness. He could not climb into a bathtub even if one was created to such a size that it fit him. So, the solution was as it remained from when the king had first had difficulty walking: buckets were filled with warm water and brought to him, and he was washed with towels and sponges.

Grimvald rarely attended these cleaning sessions. From time to time there was a matter to discuss that could not wait until after, but here and now that was not the case. Here and now, the king specially requested Grimvald's attendance, yet refused to elaborate.

So, he stood in silence. With his boots wet from the puddles upon the floor, he positioned himself to His Majesty's right-hand side and waited, hands tucked behind his back.

From time to time as he would steal a glance.

He observed Brock's grey streaked beard, how when he scratched one of his many chins his cheeks, neck, and even his shoulders would shake in a great cascade.

He saw how idly Brock would touch his bloated sides. No longer able to rest a hand on his own thigh, the king would glide his hand along the overflowing fat of his hips and ribs.

One would think that he could not feasibly move where he sat, and of course he could not go from one side of the room to the other. But when his feet were massaged by his servants, he noticeably leaned back, his stomach shifting with him a few inches as his rear took up more of the space behind him.

Grimvald had never been a romantic. Never the type to stare longingly at another reciting poetry in silence. He knew no other that he felt such devotion to other than his king. Could they ever... Be? He doubted it, he was the king's advisor, nothing more. The only thing Brock wanted from him was that unwavering loyalty, so he would give that and more. He would only steal the occasional glance, the 'accidental' touch.

"Out!" Brock broke Grimvald's train of thought with the sudden sharp, command. "I am to have a private word with Grimvald."

"Yes, Your Highness," spoke a chorus of voices as they gently dropped what they were doing and backed out of the room.

when Grimvald looked to the servants exiting through

the main doors he noticed they were part-way through cleaning Brock's inner thighs.

His gut was currently in a sling, lifted high enough that the weight of his chest was resting upon his shoulders and ribs, not his gut. It caused his neck to crease more than usual, and his breathing to be slightly more laboured, but just noticeably so, not uncomfortably.

Grimvald's ears flicked back. This was... unprecedented.

Brock didn't make eye contact when he spoke. He looked forward, head tilted upwards, he idly shifted to and fro, his gut swung side to side where it hung in the air. It was as if he was testing the strength of the sling. "I'm not interested in a discussion or any preamble, Grimvald. I am in need of relief at this very moment. You **will** satisfy me."

"But sir..." He wasn't sure what he was hearing. Had he been slipped something and it was causing him to hallucinate? This couldn't be a dream, could it? Grimvald trailed off when he spoke, leaving a silence between them, apart from Brock's heavy breaths. Even if he did, he was unsure of-

"**Now!**" Brock Barked.

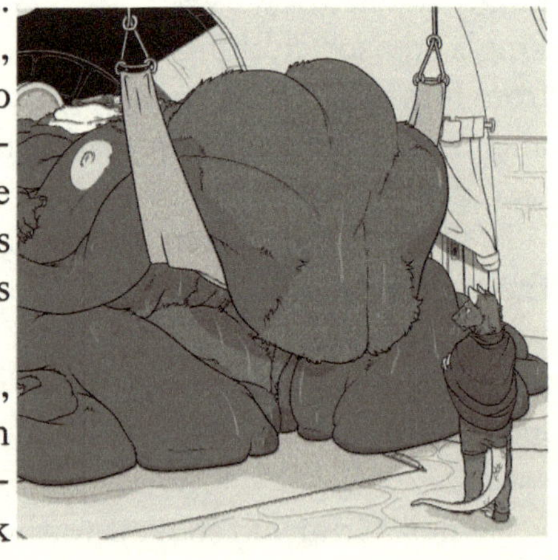

He had no choice, even if he didn't **want** to do this. Grimvald started to walk round to face Brock, rolling up his sleeves and unlatching his scabbard from his side.

Unlike other kings, Brock possessed no harem or upheld any relationships, no suitors to speak

of, just...

"Has it always been me?" Grimvald said, stopping two thirds of the way to where Brock's gut was lifted. "In those scant few moments others spoke of your relations, when you were not there to object, I overheard rumours of a time you spoke of a fancy while drunk. So... has it...?"

"Grimvald. Now." Was Brock embarrassed? No. Too proud? Maybe. His advisor who had stood by him for all these years, the only one who could read his thoughts from a glance at his face, could not see his expression now of all moments. Somehow, he knew. But Brock was not ready to discuss it. Maybe he would never be. Or even, maybe he never should be. The scandal of worthy blood on Grimvald's behalf would cause so much strife in the kingdom.

So he stayed quiet, he faced the king, and made his first moves at turning fantasy into reality.

Of course, Grimvald had visualised this happening very differently many years ago. He thought of Brock approaching him in their improvised war room on the field, of the king noticing his excitement, of surprise turning to curiosity as he took the rat right there. Letting Grimvald touch His Majesty. Letting him be used for his divine pleasure.

He **liked** being useful. He **loved** being a solution. He **adored** being all the king **needed**.

So when Grimvald lowered himself to his hands and knees he did not do so out of obligation. He did so because every night he thought upon this possibility and assumed it could never happen.

It took a few feet of crawling to reach what Grimvald assumed to be the king's loins. While he had thought upon this situation, Grimvald had of course never seen anyone so large, or, for that matter, the king's crotch. Almost like a second stomach, a massive but incredibly soft and heavily-furred mass hung. As he made contact, back arched against the pressure of Brock's underbelly, both of his hands felt across the mass.

He heard somewhere the faint sounds of the king letting out a content grumble.

Grimvald noticed he'd been holding his breath. Calmly, he took a small breath inward. He was of course met by a strong, strong assault of the king's musk. The servants had only just started on this area, leaving His Majesty with the smell of half a week's sweat and natural scent hanging on to thick fur and stagnant water.

While it was unpleasant at first, Grimvald was used to how the king smelled from multiple month long excursions and quickly adapted as he began to explore under the pad of fat squished between Brock's thighs. It took him some strength to wrest the mass away from where it stuck to the floor and surrounding skin. The jostle in fact caused a small ripple to make its way around the rest of the king's form.

He reacted with another noise, a small moan that sounded as Grimvald found what could only be described as a hole in the mass of fat, beyond which he found looser skin that, when touched, confirmed Grimvald's suspicions.

With little hesitation he pushed the soft and pliable fat inwards and out some with both paws, revealing an inch or so of Brock's cock, already hard and twitching with impatience. He attempted for a second to push further before realising the sheer weight he faced was too much for him to handle. That, or it could not be compressed any further.

But it was enough, and convinced him to toss aside his reservations before it was too late to do this. Grimvald leaned forward and ran his tongue from what he could reach of the shaft of Brock's cock up to the head and up once more onto the fur and partially exposed skin of his fat pad. He listened to confirmation that the king did not object, and after a trembling moan he lowered his head once more, tasting the sweat and feeling the heat of the man whom he idolised. From the stomach above, the legs to his sides and the pelvic mass against his forehead it was like he was being embraced, a comfort that convinced Grimvald to skip any further teasing.

He took Brock's erection into his ready mouth, sliding his entire body forward to let him take as much as he could. His nose was pressed up against a wall of fur and flab. He retreated, then returned, letting his tongue feel across the entire length, his mouth shaping itself to the divine form. He could barely hear what was happening past the cave of badger he now resided in, but it mattered little in this moment. He could feel Brock's futile attempts to buck his hips and knew that he **craved** more.

A heat rose in Grimvald's own groin. He tried at first to ignore it out of a fear of selfishness, but fear had no more home between them.

Now, one hand on his own clothed crotch, the other on the hanging fold of sensitive skin where Brock's balls once were, Grimvald continued, hearing the hiss of air from the sides of his mouth, feeling Brock's cock throbbing within his mouth, letting himself get lost in the motion, in his own desire.

It didn't take long, likely due to the king's aforementioned desperation to cum, for his mouth to be filled by the much larger man in what felt like an instant. He of course swallowed heavily when given the honour.

Brock's heavy gut **heaved** above Grimvald's head from how he panted. After a shaky moment the rat began to exit, feeling his own loins bulge against his breeches when he stood on the other side. He himself panted for a moment before an attempt to straighten his clothing.

The king looked as if he was about to say something a moment before Grimvald walked around and into his sight, perhaps how obvious it was that his advisor was also feeling the need for satisfaction. So, when in arms' reach, Brock took Grimvald's shoulder in his hand and pulled him closer. Through heavy breaths he said, "You may relieve - yourself in my presence-" He huffed again but did not speak. Instead, he motioned Grimvald away.

He understood, Brock had just been washed, what a shame it would be to sully his fur again.

The king watched as Grimvald unlatched the lowest buttons in his vest and coat before sliding a paw into his breeches. He took a step back towards the king, who did not object as he took a handful of fat from Brock's side in his other hand. Oh so gently he took care of his now fully rigid shaft. With his eyes closed he did not notice the intensity of the king's gaze. No offence to be found, not here, but a deep-seated pleasure at the realisation that Grimvald well and truly enjoyed what Brock was doing to himself, the lengths he was going to.

He wondered when Grimvald understood. What had changed? He knew that his advisor had taken some time to accept the new reality, but when did it turn into a mimicry of **his own** hunger for more?

8. Justice

No king is ever **truly** safe. Many of King Hagan Brock's own ancestors and relatives had been taken from this mortal coil by assassins, revolts, poisons, and coups.

But Brock had never feared such action from his people. With a respect earned through a healthy mix of fear and well-earned trust, no higher up in the kingdom has ever thought of usurping a badger of such renown. Or, at least, opened their mouths without swiftly suffering some form of punishment from their peers.

Most monarchs would make use of taste testers before meals to assure themselves safe from dangerous substances. But Brock, as all in the castle knew, did not employ such an individual. No, he put great trust in his personal cooks, Shiloh coming from a large family that had been loyal to the crown since the earliest days of the Brock family rule. While the Thistlestings were found everywhere in the kingdom as investors, inventors, and manufacturers, Shiloh was different. With parentage which served as castle stewards, her interest in the ingredients arriving from foreign shores delighted Brock's previous chef, leading to her education within the castle walls.

A wavering in her faith was definitely unwise. She was built by this kingdom, down to the smallest shards of bone; her entire family tree could be felled by a stumble in favour.

So she kept up her facade of satisfaction, for days, months, so long that she barely remembered what life was like before the feast.

She was the backbone of this operation: every recipe, menu, order, it was written by her. Each and every dish checked over by her own two eyes. No day was the same, and no dish fell below the standards of royalty. Shiloh would rather see herself dead than witness her dishes even **slightly** dip in quality.

So when the kitchen grew in size, with more staff, more ovens, grills, storage, it had been no issue. She had been doing this non-stop, never missing a beat. What was a dozen more heads to account for?

Even when the kitchen had to move into a hall to allow the room to be expanded she did not mope or grumble because in the end it just made her job easier! Being afforded more space to work, to watch over all in her employ, was practically an honour.

But what she did mind? What brought her blood to a boil?

Shaw.

Shaw, unlike Shiloh, was given many a boon by the king. Perhaps just by virtue of visibility, the royal apothecary was fed riches by the spoonful for keeping the king drugged. This seemed to give Shaw some elevated sense of importance as she entered Shiloh's kitchen and made moves to spike a cauldron of beef and onion stew that was being prepared.

Shaw, of course, was swiftly met by Shiloh's cane which, when it collided with her hand, produced a large 'SNAP' that made every cook flinch.

"Woah!" Shaw exclaimed, ears tucking back as she fumbled to keep a hold of the sizeable vial in her paws.

Shiloh scoffed. "Woah indeed, Shaw. What the hell do you think you're doing in my kitchen?" She promptly struck her cane against the floor before leaning upon it, the dull thud caused several shocked cooks to resume working.

Taking a step back for safety, the alchemist tripped her words into a jumble for a moment before calming and trying again: "Well uh, to make a long story short, the king made more requests for elixirs. One of them took us some time to develop. Not by me, mind you. The honour of the breakthrough goes to a fellow named Hyd, who, uhm..." Shaw was a good two feet shorter than Shiloh and had a hunch from years of craning over her work, so was a little more than intimidated by the rat before her.

Shiloh tapped the floor, the note of impatience ringing true and the message received by Shaw.

"Well, he's not returned from a meeting with His Majesty. I **assume** he was gifted something and then left the castle with a big bag of gold." Shaw gave a nervous laugh but quickly continued when she noticed the disgruntled look upon Shiloh's face. "Oh, yeah! Wrapping up, the king ordered that I immediately add the solution to his next meal! The stew would be perfect due to the-"

"Nope." Shiloh interjected.

"Nope?" Shaw replied, a bewildered smile creeping onto her face.

"Fantastic, I'm glad we've come to an agreement." Her false smile was obvious and made the other woman uncomfortable. "Now get the fuck out of my kitchen."

With a quick nod Shaw scurried away as quickly as she could. This was the last Shiloh saw of her. In fact, it was the last Shiloh **wanted** to see of her.

There was nothing more offensive to her than the idea of some idiot from another part of the castle messing with **her** food.

In the dark of the night a storm howled outside. Great terrifying winds spooked livestock away from the safety of their steading and tore trees clean from their roots.

But inside the castle it was quiet. The great stone walls did not budge. No gusts of wind interrupted the sleep of any who dwelled within.

Well, except Grimvald.

While the king slept in the throne room he was surrounded by plush luxuries and the sound of his own strained snoring. The other servants dwelled deep within the castle's bowels, no windows for rain to patter against or shutters to clatter in the night. That honour was for Grimvald alone. In his tower high in the sky he swore he felt the flooring sway, but it could've just been his own nerves.

He knew at least that some slate tiling broke free from the ceiling by a definite smash of something hard against one of the castle walls, followed by a constant drip of rainwater falling from the ceiling.

He couldn't stand it. Lying awake at night was torture, left alone with nothing to do except stew upon his thoughts.

So, he stood, donned his working clothes, his belt, blade, boots, and descended from his high tower. Though he was just going for a stroll within the confines of what was technically his own home, Grimvald still upheld his values at all times. He must present well, even if he had no audience.

Of course, he continued to be consumed by his own

thoughts as he walked, thinking on the trials of the day and all that would need to be tackled tomorrow. Of shipments, visiting entertainment, nobles, how the railings needed to be adjusted yet again to accommodate the dwindling mobility of the king's arms.

Oh, how little distraction the halls provided. Not a soul was encountered, every tale was told by the images upon the walls and every room without a purpose to frequent was as old news as they ever were.

It took a few minutes longer before Grimvald came to a realisation. He was turning a corner when he stopped. Not a soul... What of the guards?

His eyes went wide, his half-dazed state due to the sleepless night was shoved aside as he hurried his pace forward. Surely he had simply walked the halls in-between shifts? Surely...

When he did not encounter any guards after entering one of the main halls, Grimvald was truly suspicious something was wrong.

He picked up his pace once more, a quick march towards the guard's armoury, usually where soldiers were seen guarding the standard polearms and armour. Instead, nobody was to be found. Not far from there he could hear a **clattering**.

Chains, metal against metal, thudding dully on the wood floors. Grimvald dashed around the corner to a hall that led on to the barracks and servants' quarters, which is where he finally saw the problem.

Someone had wrapped a large heavy chain, and a common smoke house lock was preventing anyone inside from leaving. At a glance, Grimvald saw the chain itself was heavier than he could lift on his own.

He heard another thud, then a muffled voice.

'Hello!?' He assumed the person on the other side of the door was trying to say.

He approached, placing his ear on the door's edge. There were several chattering voices.

Grimvald shifted to speak through the keyhole. "What happened? Why are you locked in there?" His desperation was obvious, as well as his frustration.

The guard spoke up again, clearer this time. "Sev'ral of us were walking the halls when we saw the other doors down t' here were barricaded. We grouped, n' followed procedure, but a band of intruders jumped us from a servant's hall! Next thing I knew we were kicked down the stairs n' locked in here **sir!**"

Grimvald tried the chains again. Between the weight and how tightly they were bundled they barely budged.

That's when he realised what the intruders would be after.

Without another word the rat darted away from the door and down toward the castle's main halls, flinging himself 'round corners and toward the throne room.

Two hooded lanterns shone through peepholes of focused light within the grandiose throne room. The beams swept in great arcs, glancing reflective surfaces of decorative metal and barely registering silks more expensive than the spending of every rat that had invaded this room.

A concentrated force, four of Dachstaat's finest soldiers were equipped with jack chain armour, breastplates and helms. They gripped deadly arms tightly, those without lanterns kept pole-arms at the ready, those **with** kept blades at their sides, longswords of the finest craftsmanship.

They were ready. Having found passage through the loading doors the four rats crept under cover of the storm.

They had tricked the king's guard with their knowledge of protocol and military passcodes, and they had found their goal, and strangely enough it was here.

He was here.

The king had hidden himself away in his throne room, likely a cowardly move to buy himself time in the face of death. But soon he would have no fear, they thought to themselves. With the king dead this era of 'peace' would end, and the common people would be free from slaving away day in and out without a leader to give them hope for something more. No, the king would hide no longer.

With a great sweeping motion the swordsmen drew back the massive partition curtain and shone their lanterns forth into the dark.

But the spear wielding soldiers paused.

All they could see was a big dark... something.

Their lights moved with less certainty this time. They moved to the side, both to the left. The dark pile to the untrained eye could've been a pillow, or perhaps a large fabric draped across a pile of stuffed bags. There was a lumpiness to the form and a small protrusion like part of the fabric had been tied into a knot and now sank back into itself.

The two rats with polearms twitched and lowered their weapons ready to move when they noticed something in the pile move. Upon further inspection by the two holding lanterns, the small knotted lump moved and the rest of the shape shook in response. While one kept their light upon the knot, the other moved to slowly scan the rest of the mystery, which is when the entire scene began to take shape. The knot was in fact a foot, one so swollen with fat that it was barely recognisable alone, sinking uselessly into a plush ring of lard that was not too far away from swallowing it.

Further up and along, a massive expanse of belly fat

extended so far that even if the thing's hands could reach past the drooping chest, they wouldn't be able to lift the gut without the majority still lying heavily upon the floor. Even further up many rolls and layers of neck fat framed a face. A face with eyes that squinted from cheek-fat squishing upward, and ears that similarly sat higher than they naturally would. A face that glared and bared sharp off-white teeth down into the darkness.

"**Guards!!**" King Hagan Brock called out, loud enough that the present soldiers felt a shake in their armour. But, of course, none came when he beckoned.

The soldiers, who looked fearful for only a moment at the strange sight before them calmed and lowered their defences. They observed how the king's arms were so weighed down and surrounded by fat that he could not budge them, only his forearms and sluggishly at that. He could swing no sword and definitely not dodge one. They took steps forward.

"You best think twice peons." Brock spat as he spoke, thick with dinner's grease. "If you dare wander too close, I shall have all of you crushed and quartered! How dare you interrupt my sleep, intrude upon my castle, and look upon me with your sneering crooked mugs." He was more than a little angry. In days gone by these rats would be little more than grime underfoot.

But now? They laughed. At least two of them fully tossed aside any thoughts of fighting and laughed! One of them, smiling, was well composed enough that he called out his retort.

"You? What could you even **attempt** to do? You are a useless pile of hog's lard taken guise as a leader! Perhaps if I can draw blood from your swollen neck, I might make some use of you. Black pudding, perhaps!"

"I assure you," replied Brock in a grim growl, "I will be the only one indulging tonight."

Sparks flew in the darkness as the clashing of steel upon cheap iron was heard. A dagger cut through the lantern in one of the swordsman's grips and cut upwards until the hand was sliced in twain. With a pained yell the swordsman dropped the lantern, glass smashing as a sudden burst of light from oil igniting heralded a second yell. The left-most soldier wielding a spear did not at all react fast enough to the blade piercing his neck, which all knew by the gurgle his exclamation devolved into.

In the low light provided by the scattered oil fire, Grimvald only paused for a single sharp breath inward before rushing at the two closest targets. The remaining spearman and injured swordsman were quickest to attempt retaliation, but Grimvald was counting upon their foolhardy charge. The incoming spear was deflected deftly by the advisor's doffed cape, the thick fabric hemmed with chain for occasions such as this. With a swirl around, it tied up the spear and knocked the soldier off balance, letting Grimvald turn his momentum into a quick spin that allowed his tail to lash out against the swordsman's injured hand. With the swordsman fumbling his assault, it allowed the quicker rat to riposte and knock the second invader off balance.

Both scrambled to regain their composure, so finishing them was a swift job. Grimvald grabbed up the sword for himself once his opponent was too dead to use it.

By the nature of the fight, one combatant had been given time to slip away. Out of instinct the advisor looked to the large doors to his back but only saw inky darkness. When he looked back to the king, there was a twitch to his nose, one of frustration that he did not let himself turn into fully-blown anger, lest he do something foolish.

Having crawled upon the king was the final soldier. The fool had abandoned his lantern and held his blade against Brock's neck. He was upon his knees which sank heavily into the king's shoulder, causing Brock to wrinkle his nose in pain from the pressure. The intruder laughed sickeningly, the desperate cackle of a man who knew he was not long for this world. Who was desperate to do **anything** with the moments he had left.

"**Grimvald,** you rascal!" He gripped the sword tightly, not letting it slip despite the sweaty surface he balanced upon. "If I had known you were still under the king's personal employ I would've killed **you** first! Three of Dachstaat's best, felled by one rat. You haven't changed at all."

Grimvald didn't recognise this louse. From where he stood, he could barely even see him. With the arc of Brock's stomach and the size of his chest, plus even how that chest and stomach heaved and shifted with each breath... He did not want to risk hurting Brock by throwing his dagger, so he stayed silent, knowing that if he made a move this fool would strike first.

"If only you had the sense to join us! We could have ushered in a new world together! But now, I'm going to have to kill you-" The intruder stopped, his rant punctuated by a sickening crunch. Then the sound of thick fluid pattering upon sweaty fur.

Grimvald could barely see what was happening. In a moment of distraction, the king's mouth had closed in on the soldier's sword arm and now had taken the wrist, arm, and shoulder of the rat into his mouth. Metal, padded leathers, skin, and bone all. They were pierced by Brock's finely honed teeth. The strength of his jaw was without equal; that much was clear by the blood-curdling scream the rat let out when Brock bit down even harder.

The sword dropped out of the soldier's grip, rolling and landing in the crease between Brock's gut and the flat of his chest. Following that was a gout of blood from the king loosening his grip for but a moment. It was not a kindness, no. Like a wild animal he lunged again to take more of the rat into his maw, what he could move of his left arm pushing the soldier further into his mouth.

With a savage pull, he used his teeth to rip great gashes into the soldier's chest and shoulder, then let go, letting him drop onto his chest and roll down onto the ground, bouncing on the way.

The king took long, deep breaths. His entire form seeming to rise and fall.

"Y-Your Majesty," Grimvald said, composing himself. "Shall I retrieve the guards?"

Brock grunted, seemingly trying to move to better see the other. In response to that Grimvald took a step back. "No. I'm not done with him."

Grimvald was confused but kept his tongue still. The soldier at his feet was still twitching but was not long for this world.

The king spoke again. "Remove his armour, bring him back to me."

It was a strange order but not one that Grimvald had any say upon. He did what he was told. He removed the soldier's breastplate, helmet, shin and jack chains, then further took off any padded clothing, gloves and shoes. He then tied the soldier to one of the ropes that connected to a railing above and used the system to bring him upward.

"Come." Brock said simply.

Grimvald was already prepared to but only moved when told.

He had never climbed atop the king, this was a first, something that he'd not even imagined himself doing. To step upon a king? He felt offended toward himself with each and every movement. But to go against Brock's orders? That surely outweighed any doubt.

So, he did his best to avoid putting pressure on Brock with any single hand, foot, or claw. Using shins and forearms, as well as the ropes he made his way up to see Brock face to face.

"Once again, Grimvald, you saved me," Brock commented, pointing a thick finger towards the other. "But I cannot let this happen again. As much as I enjoy watching you outwit combatants." Brock's grim expression shifted into his usual toothy grin when Grimvald came into his reach. Without hesitation, the king took Grimvald by the arm and pulled him close, letting his mouth envelop the rat's.

Grimvald tasted many things in that moment, a wealth of the day's flavours were enveloped by a coating of fresh metallic blood. It was slathered over Brock's face and soon similarly coated Grimvald when they kissed.

It didn't last long. He knew why, he could of course see it in Brock's eyes. He was hungry, oh so very hungry. As he always was.

Wordlessly the rat swung the still-convulsing body closer to his king. With one hand holding onto Grimvald, Brock was overcome by his carnal needs and lunged forwards as much as he could, taking a massive mouthful of the dying rat, the entire head was in the badger's mouth. Then with another chomp, the shoulders, the torso, again and again, crunching and leeching blood as he went. In no time the barely conscious body slid heavily and awkwardly down Brock's throat.

It was monstrous.

But it made Grimvald's heart flutter with excitement.

9. The New Staff

Shiloh was never to see the light of day again, or even hold another spoon. The investigation into the invasion of Castle Hordrigg that night was shortened considerably after one of the staff reported overhearing Shiloh's displeasure, plus the fact that there were no signs of forced entry to the outward facing padlocked pantry doors.

Grimvald, of course, held the final say. So, like a heron above the water gazing into the dark below, his patience paid off in one swift strike.

But of course, the final lingering stench of her bitter scorn, the issue of who would run the kitchen was the topic of the next day. Promoting one of the existing chefs was not advisable. If they were at all sympathetic to Shiloh's plight it would be madness to roll the dice.

So instead, a competition was held.

Seven chefs from around the country were invited to present five courses of whatever they proposed was worthy of a king. The idea was that whoever won would become the new head chef.

Unfortunately for those who value simplicity, His Majesty enjoyed every dish so much that every entry was deemed the 'winner'. Therefore, all of the chefs were brought on – at first one at a time, invited to host the feast in their own style, then two or more at once when the renovation and expansion furthermore of the kitchen was completed.

Many new dishes met Brock's palette over the coming months. He was introduced to mouth-watering curried meats, a wealth of golden-brown fried goods, and no end to innovations in the art of baking.

But as much as Brock enjoyed shoving plate after plate of food into his willing maw... a day did come when he couldn't. As Grimvald came to learn, even with Brock's monumental strength, a limb has a limit to how much it can bend when surrounded by lard. Day by tiring day, the king's forearms were restricted bit by bit. At first a bit of momentum from His Majesty was all that he required to feed himself from the tables suspended within reach. But those tables were moved closer and closer as the king was eventually unable to reach his own mouth.

There was a terrifying rage-induced roar that filled the throne room when a panting and sweating Brock was unable to reach his lips, his hand filled with cake and buttery icing. His frustration was short-lived when he realised he could extend his tongue to lick up to the first knuckle of his fingers, but Grimvald knew this was only a bandage upon the broken leg of a problem they were having.

At this point the rails had extended into a system of walkways around the king. They were secured to the castle walls to allow those operating the pulleys and such to better see what they were doing over the mountain of badger fat.

Servants were not permitted to talk to Brock upon these walkways. Obviously, this was to avoid the elevation appearing like an elevated stature. But there were exceptions, namely Grimvald, who used the vantage point to organise possible solutions.

Since His Majesty detested being walked upon it was not attempted. Instead, servants were suspended and pushed closer, hands full of various delights. That was particularly messy, and the speed at which the king required feeding resulted in multiple dropped dishes, ones that he was quite keen to eat, so he quickly grew too frustrated to give the servants a chance to practice the aerial manoeuvrers.

The next potential solution was to arrange the suspended tables in such a way that servants could stand upon them. With a quick mock-up of the layout set up, a staircase allowed dishes to be walked straight to his mouth. Unfortunately, the issue here was not that dishes would be lost, but that only so many individuals could stand upon the tables at once without risking pushing each other off, resulting in Brock becoming particularly frustrated at how **slowly** he was being fed. When they tried to remedy this by removing concern over mess or re-arranging the layout, Brock had grown so hungry that several servants were bitten, so of course required time to recover.

He needed a solution. Now.

"You're familiar with feed bags are you not, Grimvald?" spoke Archibald outside of the throne room.

He had arrived late into this whole fiasco. He was late to a great many things in fact, and in this moment only watched the proceedings from the open doors.

Archibald had, quite simply, followed in Brock's lack of footsteps. The accountant was currently sitting in a large plush chair upon a flat and wheeled cart, his legs were spread as wide as the chair would allow, and even while reclined comfortably backwards did his large, bloated gut lie upon his similarly double-wide lap. In this moment he was munching upon a vine of grapes, grunting periodically with discomfort as his belt and doublet were obviously too tight. A servant of his own sat to his side to dab sweat from his forehead and provide just about any other service he needed.

"We are **not** putting a feed bag on the king," Grimvald replied with obvious disgust.

"Oh, no, **no**. I meant no offence! To you or His Majesty. I wondered perhaps if the principle might assist you in your conundrum, sir." Archibald scratched his gut with his off hand, causing an already struggling button to snap from its threads and reveal the fur underneath. He would have been embarrassed if he had seen it or noticed anything other than the slight degree of increased comfort.

Grimvald tapped his foot. He was getting frustrated too. There was no chance this was the end.

Perhaps to himself, Archibald continued to ponder. "I suppose I saw the issue as one of biting. I suppose then there may be something in the concept of dropping the food into the king's maw?"

A beat after that, it clicked together. Grimvald's ears perked up as he marched his way back into the room. With nothing more than a swift clap of the hands every present servant backed off from their stations and stood at attention across from their king. This precise scattering of course provided Grimvald good cover to slip past everyone relatively unexamined. It wasn't **necessary** that he went unseen, but it was of course preferred that he hid how **excited** this idea had gotten him.

When he reached Brock's side (a large, plush, dark-furred mound of thigh fat) he stood close. So much so that he had little choice but to put his hands upon the badger, his hips flush with a large crease in Brock's overflowing leg.

Grimvald proceeded to speak hastily, doing his best not to fumble his words. "Sire, I apologise for interrupting your meal, but if you agree with my proposal, the kitchen can provide you your feast. Potentially faster even than feeding yourself."

Brock went to reply but paused. He unmistakably felt a point of pressure forming where Grimvald leant into him. A stiffening in his breeches that was slipping between folds of his thigh. Brock licked his lips, drooling some in anticipation.

"Go ahead." He growled after a particularly laboured breath.

"The room above this very hall shall be converted into a kitchen, additionally, a hole and chute will be installed in the flooring of that room, allowing your meals to cascade down into your ready maw." As he explained he gripped his king's leg, pressing himself further into the other's mass. "It should be easy to provide a chord for each hand so with a small movement of the wrist you can wordlessly command the kitchen to pause or resume, or the servants to move the chute. We already have the rails to install this with ease." He faked shifting his balance in place, allowing him to rub his crotch and wedge it deeper into the crevice. "Just give the word, sire."

Brock grunted, moving his leg deep within the mass of pliable fat, his entire body rippled some and Grimvald was well aware of the shift. "Get it done. **Now.**"

"You heard him! All hands to the kitchens and those who are idle will assist engineering!" The advisor called out as loudly as he could muster, which of course resulted in every rat present scattering from the room, leaving just Brock and Grimvald.

It took Brock a moment too long to realise he was left with no ability to eat, and having gone half the day with slow service... A massive growl interrupted their fun.

A second emanated from Brock's throat as he reached as far towards his stomach as he could, managing to grab a paw-full of fat from his chest.

"**Grimvald.** Feed me. They will just have to organise themselves."

On one hand Grimvald was relieved to know that Brock didn't expect him to exit this chamber so swiftly with his arousal so obviously on display. On the other, Brock **did** expect him to prioritise his king.

With a grumble held back and kept to himself, the rat walked with a slight limp and a shuffle as he made his way up the staircase of hanging platforms.

They were as shaky as he expected from watching the servants earlier. With even the slightest off-balance step they would swing away underfoot, only stopped by the next one, along which in a similar motion cascaded forth. Thankfully they were heavy enough that three or so platforms down the way wouldn't budge, but even so, Grimvald relied on crawling about half of the way toward where still-steaming dishes lay.

Once he arrived Brock simply pointed toward what he wanted with a grunt, a large bird's leg rendered unidentifiable by the thick sweet sauce slathered atop it like a shell of gelatine. He didn't dally, feeling not only the heat of the king's body below him rising, but the increasing intensity of his outward breaths accosting him hot and sharp.

He hadn't done this before, but looking upon the morsel among the similarly greasy choices abound, Grimvald had the good foresight to roll up his sleeves before grabbing the hunk of meat by the mostly exposed bone. In response, the king eagerly opened his maw, exposing his sharp white teeth, glistening gums and a tongue that lolled out lazily, expecting to catch sauce before it could drip upon his chin. The moment Grimvald extended his arm, that tongue rose to meet his wrist, almost dragging him off the platform. There was an obvious flinch from the rat when the king closed his mouth around not only Grimvald's hand, but with the length of his jaws, all the way up to his upper forearm. The king's head slowly pulled away, his teeth getting closer and closer to the skin until they scraped against the bone in his grip. The bird's flesh was pulled away easily, leaving the rat with a slobber-soaked arm and a wet, sticky bone in his grip.

While the texture of the food in his hands was not at all pleasurable for the advisor, being so close was exhilarating. He didn't bother to clean his paw. Instead, he took a crisp shelled meat and gravy pie and continued to feed His Majesty. At first by the slice, but by the third he found it much simpler to hold the whole pie in biting range and allow Brock to eat ravenously while he simply moved what remained closer and closer.

By the fourth, while Brock still obviously hungered, he did something Grimvald wasn't expecting. He took his hand between his incisors, not enough to hurt, but enough to prevent the rat from recoiling, even if he wanted to. The badger's eyes lay keenly on the expression across from him.

A grin and a narrowing of the eye that unmistakably suggested what he could do in this moment. If he chose so. There was no question about it, even without his arms, his legs, barely able to move his head, this man still had all the power in the world.

Just as Grimvald thought this to himself, as a shiver coursed down his spine, Brock jolted his snout back, pulling Grimvald down to his knees.

Now face to face, nose to nose, the badger took the initiative to kiss, their mouths wholly incompatible, so it was more akin to the larger of the two licking across the smaller's fur and mouth. He drew back from the slow embrace with a line of saliva still connecting them.

Brock spoke low. "I have grown accustomed to the libation of excess, Grimvald. I warn you I may not cease until I have devoured you."

It was a joke, he hoped. He gave out a gentle chuckle nonetheless.

Brock extended his tongue, lifting Grimvald's chin, pulling him closer, then again across his chest, until the rat knew to remove his garments and let his king handle the rest.

By the end of the day the new kitchen was installed and a hole demolished in the ceiling of the throne room. It was a simple process using the railings and platforms to erect tarpaulin and nets for falling rubble and possible slips of workers or tools.

But it was not a complex beast. It was as simple as a waxed fabric tube, a purpose made metal funnel, the fixings for each end and a system of strings to allow the king to ring bells from his position to alert the kitchen staff above of his needs.

One could be rung to pause or resume feeding, the other to change the type of food being provided - usually on a daily rotation read aloud in the morning, but sometimes, of course, a requested array of dishes. But Brock rarely had the mind or energy to provide more than solitary commands for specific dishes.

Of course, by the nature of the delivery method, many foods would not fit through the king's end of the funnel, so most were chopped finely into cubes or provided in a liquid form. This suited Brock well; he commented one day that he was feeling fuller sooner, likely due to the hastened delivery and reduced chewing this all required.

He barely ever took guests now, instead opting to stretch his stomach to the limits and feel himself grow. There was no time to speak between bites anymore.

The feast ran itself at this point. The people knew not to mess with the new regime, and other world powers were solidly put in their place. Still, Grimvald stood by his side despite the lack of mediation that needed done. That was until he couldn't, of course. Yes, day by day, he had to retreat further and further towards the walls of the room. He saw this coming. But instead of standing on one of the walkways, he allowed it to happen.

He stood back and watched as one of Brock's titanic thighs jostled less than an inch from a cold stone wall. The king's head was in the centre of the room, towards the back where his throne used to sit. Grimvald could hear him gulping some type of steak and cream-based gravy slurry. With his size, intake, and many different elixirs it was fully possible to watch him expand in real time. That is, if you were patient enough, it wasn't magic after all.

This day's feast had been going for several hours already, so his stomach could be seen large and taught bulging under layers of fat. As it rose higher, Grimvald took a step back.

Some fur and possibly some skin was grazing the wall. Brock was not alerted immediately, with so much of him about the room, a small, slightly colder patch was not immediately noticeable. But after a few minutes of further guzzling he did pause, pulling the string attached loosely to his wrist to stop the cauldron above from being filled.

He did not celebrate, nor utter more than a proud grunt of acknowledgement at the matter.

He just continued.

10. Insatiate

From inside the throne room most processes seemed almost automatic. This of course was an impossibility, but practically explained the efficiency that was on display in and about Hordrigg Castle.

The guards kept their rounds, assisting with and investigating the twice-daily shipments that came through the great gates. Beasts of burden pulled massive crates of freshly butchered meats and piles upon piles of produce. The servants moved with practised urgency, listening for new orders at all times. The kitchen (most importantly) always thrummed with activity; the beating heart of the castle had expanded outwards into several rooms with a large cauldron-like intake in the centre. They worked in several lines, each with their own prep tables, ovens, grills, and cubing stations where trusted workers cut the king's meal into easily digestible yet recognisable chunks. He refused to eat slop; he abhorred the thought. But puddings? Oh, how satisfying it was to drink upon a soup-like dessert, creams and preserves, chocolate and vanilla. When the dinner service ended, that was what the menu wrought. Multiple hours of custard by the gallon and condensed milk in every form. The king had a mighty sweet tooth, and it was satiated rarely.

As well-oiled as the machine was, no operation has a zero percent chance of incidents. Usually they were small, a leak in the food delivery tube, a delayed shipment, overworked members of staff or weights too heavy for even the castle's dozen oxen to handle. They had the means to remedy such things, which is where Grimvald found most of his workload.

On this day it had been over a week since the last interruption to the feast. It was a minor issue but a complex one to fix. See, two months earlier the original entrances to the throne room were marked as off limits, as the king's gut had expanded to such a size that it was beginning to press against the large guest doors. The worry was that there would come a point that the doors would be opened and become impossible to close again without hurting his tender skin. Thankfully, access was barely an issue. An extra staircase on the outside of the throne room was erected that lead through a newly constructed door to immediately lead servants to the walkways above His Majesty. As was tradition they were not to speak to him from this position, but this was no matter, for they were rarely permitted to speak anyway.

Those doors were once again a concern. But to be more accurate, it was the **lack** of doors. At the tail end of the king's post-dinner dessert his gut which was firmly pressing against the two massive (and barricaded) doors. As he ate there was a loud groaning, one which caused all in the vicinity to freeze. Some expected the king's bulging gut to explode! That of course was not the case, as Shaw had seen to that much, much earlier. No, the two doors were **burst** right off of their iron hinges with such force that they were thrown six feet from the archway that housed them. The sudden jolt caused Brock to shake free from the range of the feeding tube, spraying a mix of cream, fruit and custard all over his jiggling rolls.

He of course ordered the flow to be paused and demanded to know what was happening. Usually during an event such as this the situation would be explained, Grimvald would be called, and Brock would continue eating, paying no mind to the fiasco.

But strangely enough, he stopped.

He ordered one group of servants to move the tube from where it hung above him, and another to clean the mess from him.

So it was done.

By the time Grimvald arrived they were still cleaning. He was stood at the doorway after passing by the now useless slabs of finely crafted wood. What he saw sent a shiver down his spine. A massive curved surface bulging out between two solid stone walls. He walked to measure the width. One two, three... Six and a half paces.

Six and a half paces of fat and skin stretched past its limits as well as dark, dark fur that almost looked light grey due to how spread out each hair was on the lighter surface below. He reached out a paw but refrained from making contact.

Grimvald straightened himself, took a breath, and ascended the stairs to alight onto one of the walkways. At this moment several servants wore harnesses as they worked with long periscope rods. Atop these rods were spouts used for pouring warm water or to deploy wash cloths to wipe up the mess. They worked in pairs, those with water making sure to only provide so much that could easily be mopped up by their partner. Excess moisture could gather in deep folds and fester. They had not encountered this issue but were well aware of the possibility. There were times that the king needed a deeper clean, but he slept much like a rock, allowing such tasks to be done covertly.

Grimvald always savoured his first glance upon Brock on a given day. Today he had been preoccupied with several engagements outside of Hordrigg, so he took in the sights hungrily right now.

He started at the South end of the room, the unused entranceway, almost as if he was appraising the situation at hand. The king's gut filled the majority of the space in this room. From wall to wall it heaved and shook gently with each laboured breath that came from its source. It was almost like a liquid in the way that it filled the space and attempted to flow out through the doorway. At this moment there was a gap of about a third of the entranceway's height that wasn't filled, meaning his gut didn't plug up the space fully, but most vision into the room was still blocked off by badger.

At the far left and right of the room rolls of stomach and hip flowed into thigh fat. The legs were nigh unrecognisable. Grimvald had developed an eye for it and could accurately point out the soft rolls of ankle fat that completely consumed the monarch's feet. It had been a very long time since they were last seen, but it was of no consequence. He could not wiggle his toes, let alone move his feet. Above that the king's breasts rested upon his thighs. They were **each** likely the weight the king had been when he'd lost his mobility, but Grimvald couldn't be sure. Something else he was unsure about was where rib fat ended and the king's swollen arms began. Each arm ripped outwards from a central source, two hands, both close to being consumed by forearm and wrist flab. Much like the king's feet, his hands were of little function. He could move his fingers, sure, but without the ability to reach and grab anything that wasn't already in his grip he could barely move his arms more than a few inches in any direction anyway, or even get that tight of a hold, really. Even his fingers were thick and soft; they could only half-way flex. But from there, up to the roll of shoulder fat to his chins-

"Grim!" Brock barked. His speech was muffled almost; the fat of his cheeks restricted the sides of his mouth so much that now even speech was escaping him. He was a long way from uttering his last words, but at this rate there was no doubt of that eventuality.

He knew what he was being ordered to do. Grimvald called for the servants to finish drying His Majesty and vacate the room. They did so with unparalleled haste. They knew the drill.

With the door closed behind them the two dwelled in silence for a few moments.

Well, silence was never truly found in this room. The king's stomach churned, he breathed so heavily that his wheezing could be heard from out in the hall and the occasional burp was to be expected.

"Is dessert not to your satisfaction, sire?" Grimvald commented, observing the feeding tube being stored to the side an hour earlier than normal.

Brock took a moment to answer, still catching his breath from his previous exclamation. "It is. But the door... I hunger for a different flavour." He purred out those last few words. Brock couldn't truly move his head with hundreds of pounds of neck fat around him, but the subtle crease of the cheeks and straining of the eyes to look in Grimvald's direction said enough.

Grimvald's ears reddened. It had been some time since

they last shared a room without any prying eyes. Due to the nature of the king's current size and capacity, when he wasn't eating he was full and asleep only to wake and eat once more. Even when he did take a short break there would be a legion of servants cleaning or entertaining His Majesty. Grimvald should have seen it coming. He'd expected the day to come again, but still it surprised him.

He began to ask how Brock would prefer this manoeuvrer accomplished, but the king read his mind, he waved a hand in a tiny, almost fully-restricted hand wave as he spoke.

"The platforms were removed. Unnecessary." He took a breath, licking some sugary substance from between his long teeth and his lip. "You may climb upon me." His bellow was deep and carried a permission that sent Grimvald's heart racing.

He looked immediately to a ladder that had gone unused for much time, it was bolted to the wall and previously was the solitary way to access these walkways. Now it was in a good position to lower him onto the king's thigh.

He made haste, not running but putting himself in a quick and determined march to lower himself down the ladder. Five rungs down and his exposed foot paw touched fur. There was little in the way of resistance, meaning that he only had a solid step upon His Majesty after lowering himself another three rungs. He felt on one foot he could slip at any moment. The skin and fur he was upon was permanently moist with sweat and warm to the touch as moisture evaporated quickly into a barely visible haze. To be so close was an honour. To touch a god was heresy. And to walk upon one must've been blasphemy. But he was far from blaspheming; this was servitude, this was devotion, was it not?

His second foot made contact, and ever so gently he turned himself to face toward his goal. Like he had done previously when it felt to wrong, he gently lowered himself into a crawl, shins and forearms, sure to avoid any claws or pointy elbows.

All shook about him as he moved, where he applied pressure bowed and where he was became a trench. It left every roll, every divide between body parts as a great tidal wave of grey fur. In all practicality he was scaling cliffs of nondescript gelatinous flesh, a task which left his core weary. But just as his limbs began to ache, he found himself upon a plateau. The flesh did not sink about him; it was solid, a taut surface that rose above the rest like a mountain peak. The king's stomach was directly below him, and it was no exaggeration to say that Grimvald could not touch both ends of the organ with his fingers and tail if he tried. The king could fit his entire starting mass in his own gut and still call for more to fill him. Oh, how loud it was, churning and gurgling, letting off a heat which caused Grimvald to flinch when he rested there too long.

But there was a purr, a sound of satisfaction coming from the king's throat.

Grimvald spent a minute rubbing large circles on the taut area below him. The motion resulted in a gurgling of gasses being displaced, and an echoing belch from Brock a moment later. Grimvald then began his descent from the peak. It was noticeably easier to slip down folds and ridges, especially where thicker chest fur dwelled, as he had the traction to lower himself gently, at which point he had entered the territory of the king's neck. The fat here was incredibly soft. The fur was dark and any small movement sent the entire area into chaos. To prevent himself from falling, Grimvald took a break to survey the area.

At this moment he was still descending. It was gradual, but landmarks such as Brock's layered arms and titanic backside rose considerably higher than his neck, cheeks and face, which he could now see much more clearly. Or as clearly as was possible. The king's cheeks were of such a size and pushed by a cascade of neck fat (that was pushed also his shoulder fat, etcetera) that they obscured many features. His ears were only partially visible as they were pushed between his forehead and rising neck. Similarly, his eyes were forced into a permanent squint by the rising fat around him, fat which increased and eased as he moved nigh constantly by the knock-on effect of his heaving breaths. Even his snout was somewhat consumed; from below his immediate rolls of neck fat extended outward past his chin to such a point that it could be possibly pushed to cover his mouth and nose. His cheeks pushed inward to each side, and if he had the need to chew there was a constant threat of biting his own mouth due to the surrounding pressure.

But this didn't slow him, no. His eyes were still as wild and hungry as ever. Grimvald grew closer to an open, panting maw and a tongue that lolled out like a final uncompromised limb attempting to reach out.

It did not matter that Grimvald had lost his cool when his excitement rose. Brock met him with no quarrel. The two abandoned all pretence as they embraced. With one hand Grimvald unbuttoned his dark shirt, and with the other he slipped his fingers deep into a fold of Brock's cheek. As if pulling the other closer, he put some lift into his exploring hand. Brock drank deeply from Grimvald's mouth, rarely giving in to his struggle for air. The rat, crouched where he was on the king's layers of neck fat, felt himself sink where he settled, fur and flesh rising higher about him as the two kissed, surrounded by a single form, consumed by heat, the damp of sweat and the smell of the king's ever-present musk. As much as Grimvald wanted to continue embracing the other, his king spluttered, having to pant heavily as he tired in no time at all.

For a few moments Grimvald sat back, giving Brock space as he fully removed his shirt. But the king was not satisfied with this.

"I did not tell you to **stop**." He would have been a lot more threatening if he wasn't struggling so much, but his actions compensated for the deficit as Brock shoved a swallowed arm inward causing a cascade of fat to quake Grimvald's foundation and squish him in between a layer of (assumedly) chest and neck.

He barely kept his composure, letting out a quarter of a surprised yelp as he fell into the pit before him. Brock's drooling maw and tongue stopped him from laying prone upon His Majesty. Instead, an arguably more dignified position was found. The king's teeth graced his shoulder and chest, the flat of his fangs and incisors against Grimvald's skin and bone. His lower jaw similarly was upon his ribs and his tongue put force upon the skin between, licking slowly against the grain of his fur. He was soaked right through and concerned by the teeth upon his exposed body, but even as his heart rate raced the humongous badger stayed gentle. Of course, Brock was hungry; every day he ate just a little more, and that had been his normal for about as far back as he ever **cared** to remember, so he **must** have been hungry. He was not known for his willpower; he took what he wanted when it was wanted.

Grimvald had to place his paws upon Brock's muzzle and pull himself away when Brock opened his maw wider. If he had not, he would have slipped between eager teeth, and even with his effort, Brock's tongue still beckoned him closer. They were both flirting with death and Grimvald could only wonder how he was still so aroused.

With a decisive push away, Grimvald capitalised off of a moment of indignant grumbling to unbutton his trousers. Underneath tight undergarments his needy cock twitched as it strained against the stiff fabric that bound it. The king closed his mouth at this and peered down with curiosity. It took some straining to get a good look, creating an entirely new fold below his scruffy chin.

Tilting his head and smiling slyly, Brock gave a keen look to his admirer as he coaxed the other. "Let us not be wasteful Grimvald, all delights must meet my palate." When he finished speaking he gave the other no chance to reply, he licked the other through his remaining clothing, soaking him from crotch to chest.

He took no time to agree or comment upon the invitation, but did calm his own anxieties by not immediately acquiescing to the king's offered mouth. Instead, after doffing his last layer, he took a handful of cheek fat in each paw and rutted unceremoniously into a deep fold of Brock's neck. To cut short any jeering from the other he arched his back and embraced him. Brock could be felt moving somewhere under the surface, turning the waves of lard beyond them to crash like the raging sea. But Grimvald was unshaken, and he kept hold as he humped the slick fold beneath him and accepted the guidance of his king's hungry maw. When his king tilted his head upwards, he followed the order and lifted his body so that the task could be finished properly.

As if taken by his craving, Brock madly wrapped his tongue between the incomprehensibly smaller individual's legs and pulled him closer as he licked Grimvald's taint, just about grabbed his balls and finally engulfed his cock causing the startled rat to cuss as he came in Brock's mouth.

Grimvald clenched his eyes shut and arched his back as Brock licked hungrily once more, only able to fall back when Brock felt like releasing him. As Grimvald slid back down a slope of neck fat towards Brock's chest, the badger slid his tongue across his teeth to savour the moment before swallowing.

Soaked by sweat (his own and the king's) and spit, Grimvald, ever proper, felt a pang of shame for appearing so unkempt in the presence of His Majesty. Although, by the glance he was given by the king, a curious smile at the splayed-out and mussed rat, he felt some relief in the knowledge that Brock was not adverse in any way.

Brock spoke. "I know what you are thinking Grimvald," he grunted, punctuating his speech. "I may be no stranger to pleasures of the flesh. But some do not suit me well... Yet you, so entranced, have served me well." He took his breath sharply; as much as he tried to speak at length, it still gave him trouble. "Better than well. You entrusted every inch of your being to my command. Yet you yearn for nothing more than this as your reward." He gave a grim chuckle, shaking the foundation Grimvald lay upon. "You surely cannot be satisfied, can you?"

"No, sir," he answered far too swiftly, sitting up somewhere he was displayed prone. "Your Majesty, I will not be satisfied until you are."

King Brock's smile twisted into a toothy grin, it flexed the folds of cheek and neck fat that rose above his head to either side as his eyes widened hungrily.

"Then let us call upon the kitchen staff, my dessert awaits me."

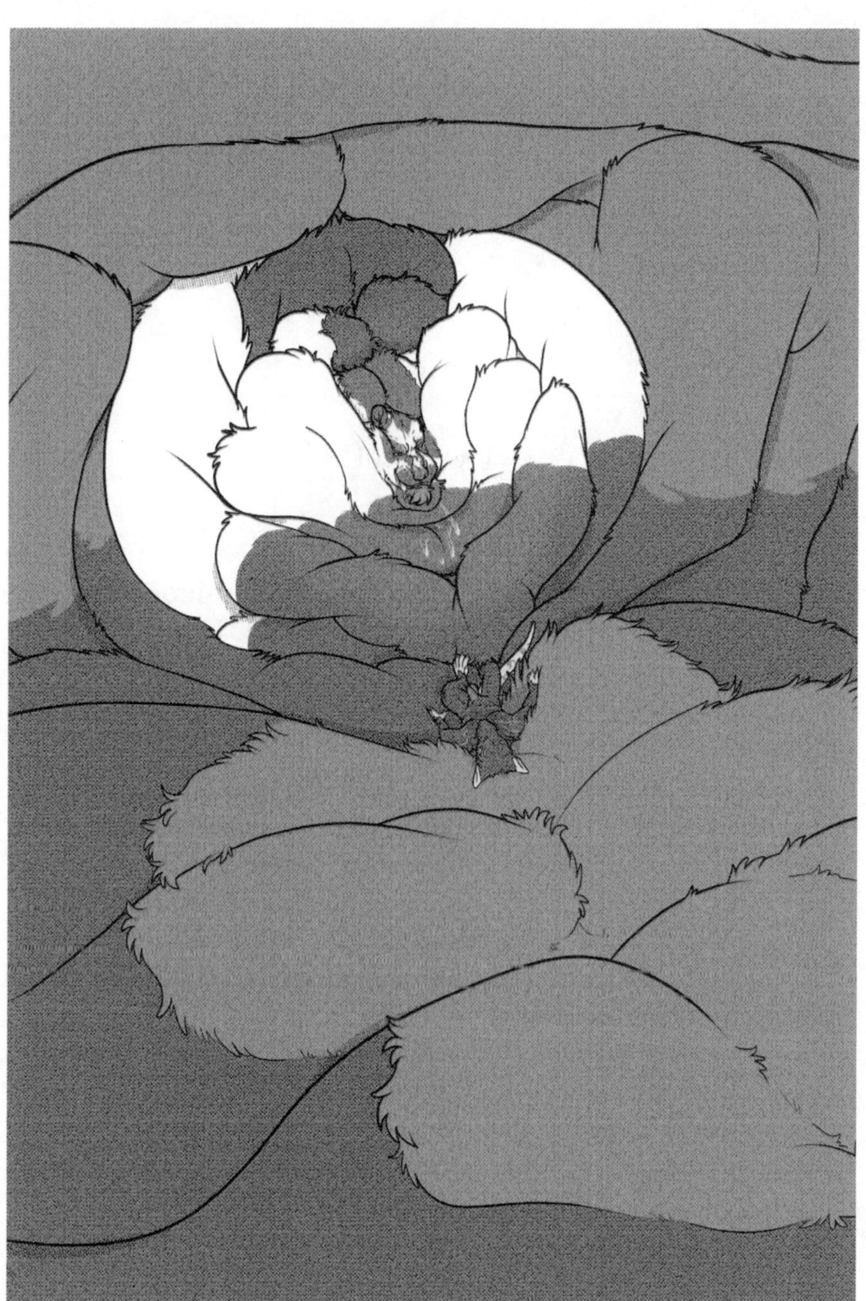

11. Moving Mountains

Much time had passed since the doors of the throne room were removed explosively from their hinges. It was a sign. Grimvald, at least, saw it as such.

As the years went on, a great reconstruction commenced. The king clearly illuminated that his size was to increase exponentially, so why court dysfunction by keeping the bones of the old regime? A king needs a castle, a fortress as a monument to his power. Hordrigg was indeed a beautiful construction, but so... small. Sure, they could knock down some walls and extend the throne room, but how long would it be until he reached the ceiling? Another three years by all estimations. Grimvald was anything but short-sighted, and Brock was anything but satisfied.

So they decided to double the size of the castle, create a throne room with the same footprint as the entire building's original foundation, and move anything unnecessary to the heart of the operation further away from where His Majesty grew. It was no small undertaking. By the time the team of architects were happy with their plan the stone walls of

King Brock's room had begun to strain from his weight, so they at least knew where to start. The structural damage was no problem; with careful planning and plenty of support beams where the stone was being actively removed brick by brick, they afforded themselves some more time. The most pressing part, of course, was the old entryway into the room. Where once there was an archway, now the open planning had Brock's gut spilling out toward the main hall, about twenty feet of extra floor space followed by a flight of stairs. Or, well, fourteen feet after his fat had settled from being previously held back by the walls.

While there was much in the way of dangerous manoeuvres to come, they were nothing compared to the next step. Part of the plan included extending the ceiling, which at the time is exactly where the kitchen operated. The only time they could move the entire kitchen without interrupting meal time was during the night. While the king was a heavy sleeper, he also expected to be fed from the moment he opened his mouth in the morning, which gave them between eight and twelve hours to move and set up not only the kitchen but the entire feeding system. Tubing had to be rerouted, the rails removed, and a temporary solution installed: chimneys for the fires quickly cut in through floorboards and walls. It wasn't pretty but it was done, and with enough time to spare that they had eggs hitting boiling water by the time the king's eyes first blearily cracked open.

The rest could be done while His Majesty was awake. But that didn't quite mean that the path ahead was clear of trouble.

"You're not seriously expecting me to okay this, are you?" Grimvald's nose scrunched in disgust at what the head of demolition was telling him. Maria was incredibly good at her job; she oversaw much reconstruction in the city and felled plenty of stone without incident or damage to surrounding structures. **But:** those structures, like any, were built to last, made to resist whatever nature could throw at them. You could easily toss a stray brick and not see a dent.

But as heavy as he was the king was not a building. Mortal or no he still wished to get through this process unharmed.

"Those walls are right above him, sir." She was no delicate bud, while her light and soft fur suggested a work-free life, she was built of sturdy muscle and an unshakable tone of voice. "We can take apart the wall by hand, in fact we are prepared to do that, sir. What we can't do is assure there won't be any accidents. If something, heavens forbid, falls from above, the safety net will stop His Majesty from being struck."

"You really expect a **net** to stop a stone that by all accounts could crush any rat to death? It takes at least three men to lift **one** without injury." Grimvald was doing his best not to get frustrated, but Maria was foolishly firm on this point. He simply gritted his teeth and pinched the top of his snout, right between his eyes.

"I'll take any alternatives you have, sir."

He took a breath, glancing over the plans. There was a note that was partially scribbled through on the same page where the plans for the net were drafted in, something about "a ramp? What's this about a ramp?" He gestured toward the scribbles.

"Not possible sir, see this angle? It's not steep enough, any stones will knock right through the wood like an arrow through paper. We'd need more space behind His Majesty." She pointed on the plans where the perfect space would be and indeed the king's rear was too high to allow the safeguards to be installed.

Grimvald replied soon after. "If he were several feet closer to the entry hall and the stairs, would there be space then?"

"Yes, sir."

He paused. Seven feet wasn't a huge distance, but for someone who hadn't moved under his own power for years it was a practical impossibility. Then again, they'd never tried anything like this before. "There's a first time for everything." Grimvald muttered to himself.

Maria's ear twitched, she dared not pry, simply standing at attention as Grimvald rolled up the documents between them and faced her properly.

He spoke with a new determination when he said: "I shall address some contacts and send a courier for you when the time comes to install that ramp." Then he departed the room to find someone who could calculate how many oxen they would need to move a mountain of badger.

Shaw ran her fingers through her curly fur, whiskers twitching as she silently jotted down her estimations. With the assumption they'd make enough yokes available, they could fit four oxen shoulder to shoulder in the main hall. This was of course accounting for space between them so they can move without treading upon each other. Therefore, with the extra floorspace provided by a somewhat sturdy temporary ramp over the staircase, they could fit 32 oxen nose to tail while providing enough space front and back for the staff to do their part. But she wasn't to think of the staff, she was to focus on skewing the numbers in their favour.

Those oxen could at most pull ninety-six thousand pounds of weight, but that was not considering the friction of pulling the king through a room he was clearly wider than, and the fact that his weight could not possibly be estimated with the mathematics of anyone present. That surely wasn't how heavy the king was, but... those oxen could **lose** this battle.

She had a plan. Shaw always had something up her sleeve. As she retreated from the gallery, gathering up her notes, she saw a great number of staff gathering all manner of materials: huge barrels being pushed in addition to great rolled-up rugs marched by on shoulders.

Everything was coming together, so Shaw in her way couldn't help but let her mind wander, visualising the event ahead of them.

Firstly, the major step to be taken was to lubricate thoroughly every surface he would be in contact with. This was easily done, and the steps were being taken to ensure they could reach deep down along his sides and make contact with most of the area underneath. The second part was a doubly useful. The king wasn't to sit upon the bare floor like some peasant, and they couldn't use logs to roll underneath or any other construction materials that they needed to retrieve again afterward. Even if it wouldn't be incredibly uncomfortable, they definitely wouldn't be able to get those back. Instead, they were preparing sleds. A great point of friction would be the direct outer reaches of the direction they were pulling him, so, of course, that meant his belly fat. Once they lifted everything, it would be placed upon the wide custom vehicles where staff would unroll carpet underneath as he travelled forward. He would be moving slowly enough that friction burn could be mitigated by a small amount of lubrication.

Then the next concern was moving the rest of his body. Because lifting the entirety of his underside was no longer a possibility, instead they were to try the next best thing and lift as much of his rear as they could; with enough force and momentum at the front the rest of him would theoretically wobble forwards. Partially a matter of pulleys and a great dependence on the stronger areas of the fortress around him, they'd use a great sling to hold aloft and push forward His Majesty's rear.

While counterweights would be used, the great majority of this would of course be powered by her oxen.

Back on track.

Shaw flicked shut her laboratory's thick blast-proof door behind her. She was enjoying the basement, it was a great deal drier than the shed and that did much good for her projects. Humidity did nasty things to elixirs that require such precise measurements; a combination of that reliability and her knowledge from years of physically assisting a king to become larger than a whale had her crafting something wickedly effective in no time.

Liquids boiling, smoke and steam dancing into the air in clouds, flowers, herbs, roots, dried dragon flesh, ape tongue, de-natured basilisk venom; there were things going into this elixir that even the learned of this kingdom would have been struck incredulous upon seeing. But within the hour she had finished the test batch and was dashing down the halls.

She knew who she was looking for, and the whelp was all too aware of the look in her eye when she spotted him. Callum had tasted the sting of her creations before. At first it was for the sake of curiosity, but as soon as he'd signed a contract he had sealed his fate as Shaw's eternal test subject.

Callum dropped the mops he was carrying with a clatter and screwed his eyes shut. She snatched him by the shoulder and despite standing a foot shorter fixed the bottle in her hands to his lips, head tilted upwards, with surgical precision and an assassin's speed.

While afraid, he stood firm, knees shaking, ears pinned

back, and eyes still closed when she retreated a safe step back to observe.

All in the vicinity, three other servants included, paused to watch, breath held in anticipation. After about thirty seconds, Shaw was disappointed. No visual changes. It hadn't worked. She tapped her foot and then her fingernails against the glass bottle in her hands.

That's when Callum opened his eyes and flinched. His fingers ached, then momentarily they felt so... light? Fuzzy? His tail twitched and felt the same. He turned to look at the others around him. When his usually frail neck grew with muscle they gasped, and one person even fled.

"Wha- Ow!" Callum tried to speak, but the act of moving his jaw caused the muscles to grow. The hand that moved to touch his aching face followed suit, his entire arm reflecting a lifetime of hard labour. After only a minute of panic and investigating his body, he no longer looked like a dishwasher but like he hauled lumber. To that Shaw practically leapt into the air, giddy with delight. "Wow Callum! Look at that!" She unlaced the top of his shirt, taking a look at his chest. In a few more moments his bony form was tough with muscle. "Just as I wanted, accelerated growth of **muscle** rather than fat. Even small movements increase muscle density during the potency period." She hopped back a step, a huge grin on her face. "Well, Callum, I must go make another thirty-two batches. See ya!" With that she dashed back to her lab.

"Wuh, wait!" Callum called out, standing still as a statue. He dared not run after her, if keeping himself standing made his calves double in diameter, what would a sprint do to him? "Wh-when does the potency period end!?"

On the day of the operation Shaw led thirty-two oxen toward the castle, Grimvald was astonished at the sight. He had not had the privilege to pass by Callum and notice his new blacksmith physique, so when those oxen were due to arrive, he had no idea what to expect. It was only yesterday that Shaw left to drug those animals and today they approached appearing as if their legs, necks, and shoulders had been inflated. But it was no trick, the muscles on these beasts rippled and flexed like any other, bulging with each easy stride.

Up until this point appropriate pulling power was Grimvald's greatest concern. Now he could breathe. Now he could begin.

On his command the hundreds gathered began to apply oils to the king's sides, belly, and thighs, they hooked up the oxen in their yokes, prepared the sling and did last minute checks on every knot. As to not make this task more difficult right now, just as the sun was rising, Brock was not being fed, so all in proximity heard the massive growl that emanated from the gut they were handling. At times from this low angle, it was difficult to even see what they were looking at as part of a person. What they were observing was simply a massive wall of grey fur.

Of course, Grimvald knew better than that. He clapped his hands and reminded everyone that they needed to begin as soon as possible so that the king could begin his breakfast with as little delay as possible. Once that was said he started climbing up temporary ladders to the second floor, finding an advantageous position to locate Brock's face and sitting there with his legs over the edge.

"Today?" The king was still half-asleep. He often was. Most of his day was spent drowsily consuming, mindlessly filling himself without a single concern. It's the only way you can fatten yourself up to such a size, cheeks so large they squish into the snout so that only the furthest inch can be seen, eyes barely registering anything past his own face, with the fat of his neck pushing forward to his forehead his ears could barely catch sound past his own sloshing movements and cavernous growls.

Grimvald knew he couldn't be heard clearly, nor seen all that clearly either, so when he nodded and called out a clear "Today," he wasn't sure if Brock heard the word so much as he read the tone. But he may have heard the others. With great gusto the groups called out to Grimvald, announcing themselves as prepared.

The pulleys were primed, sling held in position, sleds creaking under the weight of a fraction of the king's gut, and oxen held waiting to pull.

"On my command!" Grimvald called out, up in the rafters, a hand aloft, eyes darting to each position and ending up locked on his king. "**Pull!**"

With a mighty crack of ropes tugged tight and the straining of wood against them the rats gathered heaved, and oxen stomped forward to move the mighty bulk of their monarch. Despite the rippling muscles of the pulling oxen, the bulk of the counterweights lifting him, and the hundred rats doing their part Grimvald could clearly see how static the king was from his vantage point. While his backside was somewhat lifted by a combination of the oxen and the counterweights, there was an illusion of movement, the fat of his rear and back pushing forwards. But the sled was making no progress, and his core had only shifted two feet in the right direction. The moment they stop he would simply settle back again.

"We need more! Push! Push!" Grimvald called out, hands cupped to either side of his mouth. "Give it your all!"

"Heave! Heave!" a guard cried, leading a group who

were pulling with their own strength. In no time they were shouting in tandem, claws to stone, hooves creaking from the pressure. With a shove, a shake, a step of progress from the oxen the king's gelatinous body shifted ever so slightly along the greased floor.

"Keep going! He's moving!" A maid armed with a mop and a bucket of oil watching this unfold called out from the side. With that confidence all gathered kept their pace, continued pulling and witnessed as **chaos unfolded.**

The pulleys holding the counterweights buckled, the stone crumbling under the weight of the king's rear. The walls to each side of him followed suit with the new imperfections in the stone. A great crack formed and caused the room to unfold, ancient stone bucking outward in a great cascade that spread even to the unpressured back wall of the throne room, leaving the only standing constructs being the temporary supports for the upper floors and those too far beyond to be in the line of fire. But the destruction didn't end there, as the metal fixings for the pulleys flew toward the oxen, striking their flanks and causing a panic. They were stone in body but their minds were easily flexed by the pain. At least twenty of the oxen writhed free from their restraints and made a mad dash for the closest exit. Servants, guards, people of all kinds had to leap aside to avoid being trampled. As the sleds (still attached to the oxen) flew down the stairs and rode along with the animals, they brought at least five terrified rats along, either tied to the sleds or too scared to let go of them.

As the dust rose, as Grimvald shielded his eyes from flying whips of rope and shattered metal, the king shook back and forth, and as everything else did he settled... about half a foot from where he started.

Like in all matters the king was quite stubborn. Not to

be convinced, shaken off his position or, now quite literally, moved. The miracle at hand was **not** that nobody was injured by this event, no; quite a few people were injured, actually. The miracle was that the king was uninjured. He was covered in a fine coating of dust, swathed with ropes and fabrics from various sources, but otherwise nothing had landed upon him or wounded him.

In the ensuing moments as people groaned from pain, kicked, struck, crushed, coughing from the dust, the king called out: "I'll be having my breakfast now."

It was foolish in hindsight, to attempt such a task with some self-imposed immediacy. It dissuaded all organisers within Hordrigg from ever humouring the king and his movement to another location again. Instead, they hauled the stones by hand with a crew to tie each in a harness, then safely upon a crane until they were cradled away from sight of the king. It was incredibly slow, but it was done without incident – a first for an operation so precarious.

In due time the walls were expanded, the hall and stairs beyond levelled, consumed by the great arena that made up the king's new throne room. In the direct centre his head could observe the upper levels, where exposed halls and walkways in this new circular design looked out over balustrades at the glorious form of King Hagan Brock. On a floor above that, almost looking as if it was suspended, sat the new kitchens from where, of course, a feeding tube descended.

His neck and cheeks rose to meet the food source and indeed rose to surpass his snout. While there was worry he may suffocate, the pressure of smaller rolls of cheek-fat pushing outward forced any fat to naturally ripple away from his nose, so in that way cheeks flowed up to chins and neck to shoulder. There was little difference save for a layer of white, black, then grey.

Breaking the norm, heaving upwards with his occasional struggles for breath under the surface, was his chest. His nipples had disappeared under the curvature of his rising breasts, these two massive forms rose higher than any other point of the body like twin mountain peaks. Even more so than his seemingly shrinking arms, further obscured by surrounding layers of belly and hip all pushing upwards, they were forced together by thighs that spread far, reaching toward their new goal. As big as this room was, it still had walls, and Brock would surely grow to meet them.

In the mid-day the sun shone into the room from above, a stained-glass sky on the castle's roof let in a mixture of natural light and a dancing rainbow of shimmering luminescence. Gently the king's fur was warmed by the sun, sweat rising to the air as it evaporated as a gentle fog. Servants with paper fans dispersed the haze, chatting among themselves in the king's court. Their voices didn't reach past their discussion, made private by the performers above as a harp and lyre danced to and fro, song and response. The king's entertainers were perfectly positioned, amplified upon their stage by the stone curvature that backed them. It amplified downward filling the floor with their conversation, a fantastic backdrop to the guzzling of food and the churning of His Majesty's shifting mass.

As always, there was a great array of matters to attend to. Dignitaries came, admired His Majesty, and left to spread word of his latest conquest. But no matter who came, nobility, warriors, entertainers, the servants, they all left, and in the end only Grimvald remained. The halls silent, balconies emptied, he alone beheld.

The king was not the only greedy one within these

walls. Grimvald found himself making orders these days. He sought higher density of calories, had Shaw quest in search of mythical ingredients for prospective elixirs, sent warriors to new lands with vicious demonstrations of power in their never-ending need for **more**.

He was indeed greedy, but it couldn't be said that he was less or rivalled the king's avarice. Perhaps it was a shared mania, a partnership in this obsession. So here, with the moon rising and the candlelight as his guide in this solitary moment between labour and sleep, Grimvald admired their work, **their** progress. He could allow himself to linger, fingers gliding with no resistance against the outer edges of his love, heat radiating from the surface all the way to his flushing face. It was so distant now, that feeling of hopelessness he felt when the feast first began. As he gazed upward it was less a memory, more a bad dream fading from conscious memory.

This was his purpose, his life's calling. His guiding light.

Brock's conquest was far from over.

Special thanks:

Firstly, thank you for reading!

I'd like to thank my friend Casey for providing much motivation, taste testing, and being test tasted during the process of this project.

I want to give a special shout out to Denya for being such a huge inspiration and a very cool person to chat to. Much appreciation as well to Aurelina; you might not know it, but you really motivated me!

I'm honoured to have received everyone's support, including the wonderful people at Fenris Publishing.

www.ingramcontent.com/pod-product-compliance
Lightning Source LLC
LaVergne TN
LVHW091000080826
845145LV00003B/1071